Crusade of the Flaming Sword

Iola dashed into the foliage of the forest, and Joe lost sight of her. Next the knight galloped into the forest. Joe kicked his horse, pressing it on still faster. He felt his heart pounding in rhythm with the horse's thundering hooves, and soon he saw the greenery of trees rushing past him.

Up ahead, through a maze of trees, Joe caught sight of the fleeing pink gown and the pursuing black armor. Joe kept galloping after them.

Joe then saw Iola glance back over her shoulder, gauging her lead. She crashed smack into a tree trunk!

Iola reeled unsteadily on her feet. Seconds later Joe saw the knight pull up beside her, raising the flaming sword high, aiming to bring it down on Iola's gown!

The Hardy Boys Mystery Stories

Available from MINSTREL Books

THE HARDY BOYS® MYSTERY STORIES

131

The
HARDY BOYS®

CRUSADE OF THE FLAMING SWORD

FRANKLIN W. DIXON

A MINSTREL® BOOK

PUBLISHED BY POCKET BOOKS

New York   London   Toronto   Sydney   Tokyo   Singapore

This book is a work of fiction. Names, characters, places and incidents are products of the author's imagination or are used fictitiously. Any resemblance to actual events or locales or persons, living or dead, is entirely coincidental.

A MINSTREL PAPERBACK *Original*

A Minstrel Book published by
POCKET BOOKS, a division of Simon & Schuster Inc.
1230 Avenue of the Americas, New York, NY 10020

Copyright © 1995 by Simon & Schuster Inc.

Produced by Mega-Books, Inc.

Front cover illustration by Vince Natale

ISBN: 0-671-87215-X

First Minstrel Books printing April 1995

10 9 8 7 6 5 4 3 2 1

THE HARDY BOYS MYSTERY STORIES is a trademark of Simon & Schuster Inc.

THE HARDY BOYS, A MINSTREL BOOK and colophon are registered trademarks of Simon & Schuster Inc.

Printed in the U.S.A.

Contents

CRUSADE OF THE
FLAMING SWORD

1 Welcome to Avalon

"What think you of the fair so far, milady?" Frank Hardy asked.

"I think it's a great way to spend a summer day," Frank's girlfriend, Callie Shaw, replied.

"At ten bucks apiece it better be," Frank said, only half joking.

Frank and Callie were strolling through a park about fifteen miles from Bayport where a traveling medieval fair was set up for the week. They had paid at the entrance and walked down a path leading through a forest of trees before coming to a large open field.

"Get a look at that," Frank said, gazing up at a gigantic gray stone castle with five rounded towers. Fluttering from one of the towers was a large banner bearing the word *Avalon* in red letters.

1

"It's nice to see such a large crowd on opening day," Callie said, noticing the number of people walking in the same direction they were. Some of the visitors were lining up at a large tent where they could rent medieval costumes.

"Hey, look, I think a knight approacheth." Frank pointed to an advancing figure.

Sure enough, heading straight for Frank and Callie was a knight decked out head to toe in gray armor. He wore a cloth tunic known as a surcoat over the armor. The surcoat had a sunburst emblem on the chest. As the knight strode toward them, his foot caught and he tripped.

"Methinks it be a clumsy knight," Frank observed, using the flowery language of medieval times.

The knight came up to Frank and Callie and, with a bit of a struggle, lifted his visor. "Hi, guys," the knight said, revealing himself to be Frank's friend Chet Morton.

"Chet," Callie said, brushing back her blond hair, "you look so . . . well, you look so . . . knightly."

"Thanks," Chet replied proudly. "That's the best thing about this fair. All of us who signed up to be knights get armor, weapons, fight training, and some real battle experience. All for free. I guess you might say we're the main attraction here."

"Pretty impressive," Frank said, checking out Chet's armor.

"Most of it's made of strong plastic," Chet explained, holding up one arm. Frank could see that

2

there were many separate pieces strapped all over Chet's body. "The helmet is real metal, though," Chet said.

"Oh, look!" Callie exclaimed. "I see the most exquisite princess coming this way."

"Yeah," Frank agreed, "but who's the sorry-looking guy with her?"

A girl dressed in a flowing pink gown with a jeweled crown nestled in her brown hair headed their way. Walking beside the princess was another knight in full armor, a flower emblem on his surcoat. The knight's helmet dangled from his hand, and a sheepish expression lingered on his face.

"What's the matter, Sir Joe?" Frank called.

The princess and knight joined the group. The princess was Chet's sister, Iola, and the knight was none other than Frank's brother, Joe Hardy.

"Oh, nothing's the matter," Joe said with a scowl. "Except for the fact that I have to spend the next five days wearing a tin can."

"I think he looks awfully cute," Iola said.

"We're not supposed to look cute," Chet protested. "We're supposed to look brave. Dashing. Fierce!"

Joe glanced at Chet. "It's bad enough that Chet and Iola talked me into this," Joe said. "But what really tees me off is that Frank got off so easy. All he has to do is laugh at us for a few hours, then take off. I've got to spend all week in this crazy getup. I just hope I don't get picked up for recycling!" Joe, blond and six feet tall, looked at his brother, a hint of anger flashing in his blue eyes.

3

Frank smiled, his dark eyes gleaming beneath his dark brown hair. At eighteen, Frank was a year older and an inch taller than Joe, and he often felt this gave him license to tease his kid brother.

"Aw, cheer up," Frank said encouragingly. "A little chivalry never hurt a guy."

Before Joe could respond, a strange-sounding horn blew a few times. "Let's go, folks," Chet called. "It's time for the opening ceremony!"

Several hundred people were now heading for the center of the grassy field, which was flanked on one side by the castle and on the other by a lake glimmering in the midmorning sun.

"See you later," Iola called as she ran off to join a group of girls who had also volunteered to be princesses and noble ladies for the week. The princesses wore crowns and the ladies wore tall cone-shaped hats with scarves floating down from the top.

"Watch your step," a staff member in costume said as he helped a noble lady up a few steps onto a large wooden platform that stood about six feet off the ground.

Joe and Chet joined the rest of the knights. There were about forty of them, and they were forming a line opposite the platform. The knights all wore armor, with different emblems on their surcoats. Each knight wore a purple armband. They were all high-school and college-age, and they had volunteered, like Chet and Joe, to experience the thrill of being a knight for the week.

The rest of the crowd gathered in a big circle

4

around the participants, eager to witness something they had only read about or seen in movies.

"Look, Mommy," said a little boy clutching a toy sword. "Those are real knights!"

"Yes, I know, Jimmy," the mother replied with a smile.

A herald, wearing tights and a tunic, put what looked like a ram's horn to his lips and blew a few blasts. Then, in the distance, a horse and rider were seen galloping toward the crowd.

"You have to admit," Callie told Frank, "this is kind of thrilling."

"Yeah," Frank confessed, "it's better than I expected."

"Good ladies and gentlemen," the herald announced as the rider arrived, "we have been graced by the presence of our great sovereign, King Bertram!"

As the king climbed off his horse, the ladies on the platform and the knights knelt on one knee.

King Bertram was a large man in his forties with reddish hair and a jovial expression. He too wore armor, but a deep purple cape flowed down his back and a gold crown rested on his head. With an air of authority, the king made a gesture and the kneeling subjects rose to their feet.

"Fair ladies and brave gentlemen," the king addressed the crowd, "welcome to Avalon!" At once most of the visitors and participants cheered and applauded.

"I am King Bertram," the king continued. "Actually, my name is Art Growtowski, and I'm the owner of this fair. But part of what makes our fair so much fun is that over the course of the next five days we are going to enact a story for you. Each day will bring a new chapter in a stirring tale of chivalry and daring.

"In addition," Art Growtowski continued, "we have created an entire medieval world for you to explore. There's entertainment, sporting exhibitions, a mock village, and plenty more. And on Friday night, there's to be an authentic medieval banquet inside the castle. So welcome to the Middle Ages, each and every one of you!"

"Now let the adventurous tale begin," the herald called out. "The year is 1295 A.D., the country, England. The king's base of power is here, the region of Avalon. To protect his kingdom, the king has gathered the strongest and bravest men in the realm to his side."

Frank saw Chet beaming at that description. "And now," the herald continued, "King Bertram shall bestow upon these young men the exalted honor of knighthood."

The king walked over to the wooden platform, and Iola, who was playing the part of the king's daughter, handed a long, gleaming sword down to him. The herald then pulled out a scroll and began reading from it.

"Francis of Tauverny!" the herald called.

One of the knights walked toward the king and knelt before him. "Francis of Tauverny," the king proclaimed, "I now dub you knight." The king then touched the knight once on each shoulder with his

6

sword, a gesture called the *collee*. The knight rose and returned to his place as another name was called.

"Why aren't there any girl knights?" Callie whispered to Frank.

"Because you weren't around back then to insist on it," Frank answered with a grin.

"Can you believe this?" a voice nearby complained. Frank and Callie turned to see a man in a brown monk's robe standing next to them, chomping on a piece of gum. He appeared to be in his midtwenties, and Frank instantly pegged him as a wise guy.

"I've had plenty of dumb assignments," the monk continued, "but this has got to be the dumbest."

"What sort of assignment are you on?" Frank asked.

"The name's Charlie Krause," the monk replied. "I'm a reporter for the *Bayport Star*. Just got the job a few weeks ago, and it's been one stupid assignment after another. I mean, where's the news in this town?"

Frank shrugged and turned back to the ceremony. Soon all the knights, including Chet and Joe, had been dubbed. "These men before you," King Bertram announced, "are now full knights of Avalon, here to protect and preserve the peace of the land. And I hearby declare—"

Just then a rumbling noise was heard in the distance, and everyone turned to see another mounted horse galloping toward them. The ar-

7

mored rider soon reached the crowd and pulled his horse to an expert stop. The stranger's surcoat sported an emblem of a dragon spitting fire.

"Who are you that hath so rudely interrupted our ceremony?" the king called up to the stranger.

"My name is Sir Damian of Mandeville," the stranger called, lifting his visor. "And I have come to steal your precious knights."

"But why?" the king inquired.

"You have gathered a collection of great men to your side," Sir Damian replied. "But you do not appreciate their power. Here in Avalon you dream of peace and civility. You plan to use these men as mild summer days, not as the knights they're meant to be!"

"And what have you to offer these men?" King Bertram challenged.

"Great men," Sir Damian said, now addressing the knights, "if you will ride with me away from this place, I will offer you true adventure. Across the continent we shall gallop until we have conquered every square mile of it!"

"Oh, this is exciting," Krause said sarcastically.

Sir Damian guided his horse a few paces from King Bertram. "All those who wish to join me," Sir Damian called, "step over this way and I will give you the orange armband of my order. Those who wish to remain, stay meekly where you stand."

As Frank watched, half the knights walked over to Sir Damian, and the other half remained where they were. Frank realized this was part of the show. Sir Damian then handed orange armbands down to his recruits to replace the purple ones they were wearing. Chet and Joe were among the knights who faithfully chose to stay in Avalon.

"I have my men, you have yours," Sir Damian informed King Bertram. "And ere the season turns, we shall all meet in bloody battle."

"Then you plan to attack Avalon, too?" King Bertram asked.

"Avalon is the *first* region I plan to conquer!" Sir Damian answered defiantly. He pulled a sword from his scabbard and lifted it high. "Knights of Mandeville," he bellowed, "I pledge you to war!"

"Knights of Avalon," King Bertram bellowed, lifting his sword to the sky, "I pledge you to the ideal of peace!"

The crowd cheered wildly. Shouts of "Mandeville" and "war," "Avalon" and "peace" were heard, and some of the knights began to stomp their boots as they cheered.

Suddenly the cheers were mingled with frightened shrieks. Frank's gaze swung to the platform on which the princesses and noble ladies were standing. As he watched, horrified, the platform tilted crazily and the girls started to slide. Then one of the support beams broke and the platform came crashing to the ground!

2 An Ominous Note

As the crowd watched in shock, the girls tumbled to the grass, landing in a heap in front of the collapsed platform.

Several people, including Frank and Joe, rushed over to assist the girls. "Give me your hand," Joe said, helping a princess with a slightly bruised ankle. As the rest of the girls also got to their feet, it became apparent that no one was seriously injured.

"Well, it seems someone has cast a spell on us," Growtowski announced, "but thankfully everyone is all right." He gestured to Sir Damian to continue.

"Knights of Mandeville," Sir Damian cried on cue, "let us depart this place of folly and prepare for battle!" He sheathed his sword, spurred his horse, and galloped away, his band of knights following after him on foot.

"In spite of the day's danger and mishap,"

Growtowski called out, "let us be entertained!" He gestured again, and two men in brightly decorated costumes approached the crowd.

One was a troubadour who sang and strummed a guitarlike mandola, and the other was a juggler skillfully keeping three colored balls in the air. The crowd began to watch the entertainers as Growtowski and several staff members began escorting the girls toward the first-aid station.

In the meantime, Frank and Joe examined the collapsed platform. "Frank, take a look," Joe said, indicating the remaining part of the broken support beam. Joe pulled off a glove and ran his hand over the top of the wood. "Half is smooth, half is rough."

"It looks like it was sawed halfway through," Frank observed.

"Meaning you know what," Joe commented.

"Meaning this was no accident," Frank said, lowering his voice. "This stand was rigged to fall."

"Hey, look at this," Joe said, dropping to his knees.

Frank knelt beside his brother and saw a piece of parchment tacked to the remaining part of the beam. A message was written on the parchment in black ink with old-style lettering. The message read:

Though this be Avalon of great renown,
My wrath shall bring this fair soon crashing down.
          —The Knight of the Flaming Sword

11

"What did you find?" a voice asked.

Frank and Joe turned to see the monk-reporter, Charlie Krause, moving toward them. Frank quickly pulled the parchment from the beam and slid it into the back pocket of his jeans.

"Nothing," Joe replied. "We thought this might be some sort of a prank, but it seems to have been an accident."

"Accidents happen," Frank added.

"Yes, they do," Krause agreed. "But less often than people think. What was that you put in your pocket?"

"I didn't put anything in my pocket," Frank said innocently.

"All right," Krause said, a little irritated. "Mind if I take a look at this beam?"

"Go ahead," Joe answered.

Krause examined the top of the beam, running his hand over it. "Hmmm, interesting," he muttered.

Frank and Joe casually wandered away from the stand, soon leaving the field and moving through a forested area. "I guess you thought it would be better if he didn't know about that message," Joe said, once he was sure they wouldn't be overheard.

"Definitely," Frank replied. "Why start a panic before we know what's going on? Besides, you show a reporter something like that, odds are you'll see it in tomorrow's paper."

"Believe me," Joe declared, "I still remember my picture on the front page of the *Star* when that flying saucer incident happened in town."

12

"Well, we've seen the future, little brother," Frank said, "and now . . ."

"We're seven hundred years back in the past," Joe said, finishing Frank's sentence. "Look at that, will you?"

The Hardys had come out of the wooded area and into a clearing where a medieval village had been brought to life. Visitors were strolling up and down a dirt road. Booths were set up on either side of the road, and above each was a boldly painted sign.

One of the signs proclaimed Foode and Drinke, and beneath it sausages sizzled and liquid flowed from wooden barrels. Another sign announced Leather Goodes, and below it a woman was peddling leather bags, boots, and belts. Another sign read Armorer, and below it was a man sharpening a sword on a rotating grindstone, sparks flying off the blade. Staff members in costume roamed the road, greeting the visitors and answering questions.

"Let's mosey on through and see if we notice anything suspicious," Joe suggested. "Then we should have a talk with Mr. Growtowski."

"Sounds good," Frank replied as the Hardys entered the village.

Frank and Joe couldn't help stopping at the armorer's booth, where an array of medieval weapons and armor was displayed. They admired the lances and spears and shields and finally a full suit of shining steel armor.

"Did you make all this yourself?" Joe asked the man at the grindstone.

"Everything by hand," the armorer replied. "That's how it was done back then, and that's how it's done best. Next time you march off to battle, pay me a visit," the armorer said with a wink.

The Hardys continued on through the village. "I bet that steel suit's a lot heavier than the plastic stuff you've got on," Frank commented.

"No kidding," Joe agreed. "A full suit of plate armor could weigh more than a hundred pounds. It's amazing how well the knights could actually move in outfits like that."

"How do you know all this?" Frank asked, a little surprised.

"Mr. Growtowski briefed all the volunteers this morning before the fair opened," Joe explained. "He gave us the general background on the Middle Ages."

"What are the dates on that?" Frank asked.

"Basically the Middle Ages began right after the fall of ancient Rome and ended just before the New World was discovered. From 476 A.D. to 1487, to be exact."

"They're also known as the Dark Ages, aren't they?" Frank questioned.

"That's right," Joe answered as the Hardys kept moving through the crowd. "Back then, if you were strong enough to conquer a kingdom, it was yours."

Frank and Joe noticed a young woman draped in gauzy material moving down the road toward them. She had wild black hair and exotic streaks of

14

makeup around her eyes. Jimmy, the little boy they'd seen earlier, ran up to her.

"Who are you?" he cried.

The woman smiled mysteriously. "I am the Enchantress," she said. With that, she lifted her arm, turned her hand upward—and a burst of flame appeared in her gloved palm. As the crowd murmured sounds of astonishment, the fire disappeared into thin air.

"Pretty decent," Joe said.

"Yeah," Frank agreed. "Apparently there's more than one person around here with tricks up their sleeve."

Frank and Joe left the mock village and soon came to an area where three large trailers and a horse van were parked in the grass. The two horses from the opening ceremony, one chestnut, one white, were grazing nearby.

In front of one of the large trailers, several of the girls who had fallen were having their bruises looked at. A girl in a serving girl's costume was cleaning a cut on Iola's arm with alcohol.

"Ow, careful," Iola said, wincing.

"I'm sorry," the girl apologized.

"You know how these princesses are," Joe joked, joining them. "They can be awfully temperamental."

"Well, after all," Iola kidded back, "we *are* royalty."

"I certainly don't feel like it," said a noble lady holding an icepack to the side of her face. "I'm supposed to be the daughter of a duke or something. Instead I get a black eye. One more stunt like this and I'm out of here."

The serving girl was now taping a bandage to Iola's arm. The girl was tall and slightly awkward, her costume consisting of a brown skirt and a white blouse coming off the shoulders. Joe figured she was about his age.

"Do you work for the fair?" Joe asked the girl.

"That's right." The girl spoke so quietly, Joe could barely hear her. "I've worked for Avalon the past three summers. I perform in the horse show but the rest of the time, well, I play a servant."

"I'm Joe Hardy."

"I'm Carla," the girl said, too shy to meet Joe's eyes.

"Excuse me," Joe said, noticing Frank signaling to him. Frank was standing next to Growtowski, and when Joe reached him, they followed Growtowski into the trailer that served as the Avalon office on the road.

Inside the trailer, Growtowski sat down on a sofa and began to examine the ominous note the Hardys had found.

Joe glanced around the trailer. It contained a kitchenette, a large trunk, and a computer system with a large screen that curved outward at the edges. He looked back at Growtowski and noticed a cloud passing over the man's jovial face.

"Well, chances are it's just a one-time prank, right?" Growtowski finally said.

"Very possibly," Frank responded. "But the note

does hint at further danger, and we wanted you to be aware of that."

"You didn't tell anyone about this note, did you?" Growtowski asked.

"No," Frank replied.

"We thought it best to keep it quiet," Joe added.

"You boys were pretty sharp to figure out the stand was tampered with," Growtowski said. "I wish all innocent bystanders were as concerned as you are."

Frank looked at Joe. Joe nodded.

"I'll level with you, Mr. Growtowski," Frank said. "My brother and I aren't exactly innocent bystanders."

"The truth is," Joe confessed, "we're detectives."

"Is that a fact?" Growtowski said, obviously skeptical. "And you've solved a few cases?"

"Yes, sir," Joe boasted. "More than a few."

"My brother's not too modest," Frank put in, "but he's right."

"Well, then," Growtowski said, "perhaps you boys will help me keep an eye out for trouble."

"We'll be glad to," Frank assured Growtowski. "But do us a favor. Don't tell anyone else here that we're detectives."

"Of course not," Growtowski replied. Joe could see the man was still not sure how seriously to take the Hardys.

"In the meantime," Frank said, "let's just hope there are no more accidents."

Suddenly the door to the trailer opened and a tall man in his midthirties entered. His pants and shirt were black, and he wore a colorful scarf tied around his neck.

"Perhaps it wasn't an accident at all," the man said, his gaze piercing. "Perhaps those damsels got exactly what they deserved."

3 The Wizard and the Warriors

The man walked to the computer and snapped his fingers. Instantly, liquid blue waves began flowing across the curved screen.

"What do you mean by that comment, Alvin?" Growtowski asked the man.

"I was joking, of course," Alvin replied, his piercing gaze turning into a mischievous twinkle. "But the truth is, many of the girls were talking and giggling during the ceremony. Behavior like that destroys the illusion we're struggling so hard to establish. In other words, it bugs me."

"Frank, Joe, meet Alvin Sing," Growtowski said. "He's the general manager of the fair."

Frank and Joe both said hello, and Sing nodded back at them as he sat in a swivel chair by the computer.

"These boys were just telling me," Growtowski continued, "that, uh, well . . ."

"We were just telling him," Frank said quickly, "what a great fair Avalon is. In fact, the reason my brother and I are here is that we're doing an article about the fair for the summer edition of the school newspaper. Joe's getting the inside story on what it's like to be a knight, and I'm, well, just taking in everything else."

"Alvin might be of some help to you," Growtowski said, playing along. "He's one of the few people who work for me year round at the home office in Connecticut. Most of the staff just come on board for the summer, when the fair's actually in progress."

"What exactly does the general manager do?" Joe asked.

"A lot," Sing replied, shuffling through a stack of bills. "I oversee most of the details of the day-to-day management. Like paying these—which are late." Sing waved the bills significantly at Growtowski.

"I know, I know." Growtowski sighed. "I'll figure it out later. Somehow."

"And I also do much of the creative planning," Sing continued, returning the bills to the desk.

"Alvin's one of the few people who knows more about medieval times than I do," Growtowski said.

"The medieval world is truly fascinating," Sing observed, the blue waves on the computer screen still flowing behind him. "The Middle Ages signals man's passage through the dark into the intense light of the present."

"Speaking of the present," Frank said, "that's quite a computer setup you've got there."

"Thank you," Sing replied. "I built it myself."

"Alvin's an absolute wizard when it comes to computers," Growtowski offered. "He's got every facet of the fair, from food to finances, mapped out inside that big box there."

"If you boys need help at some point," Sing said, "I'll try to oblige. If I'm not too busy, that is. So much to think of, so much to create."

Sing snapped his fingers again, and the computerized waves were instantly replaced by the words WHERE WOULD YOU LIKE TO GO? Sing's fingers began flying across the keyboard and data scrolled across the screen.

Just then a blast from the horn was heard in the distance. "That horn's for me," Joe announced. "They're calling the knights to assemble."

"I think I'll tag along," Frank said. "It was nice to meet you, Mr. Sing. And Mr. Growtowski, maybe we'll talk more later."

"I'd love to," Growtowski said with a wave.

Frank and Joe left the trailer and began jogging back toward the open field. "What did you think of Sing?" Frank asked his brother.

"Brilliant. Interesting. A little creepy," Joe said.

"Someone to keep an eye on, at least," Frank noted.

"Which I'll do soon enough," Joe said, pounding his armor. "But now it's time for me to fight!"

21

Soon the Hardys reached the field and Joe headed for the center, where the other knights were gathering for their first training session. Frank hung around to watch, along with a number of other visitors who were apparently welcome to observe. Frank noticed little Jimmy brandishing his toy sword as he waited beside his mother.

"All right, listen up," a man in armor addressed the congregation of knights. "I'm Steve Bledsoe, the Avalon staff member in charge of training you knights." Bledsoe was big and blond with a mustache, and he had a friendly way about him. Frank noticed the dragon emblem on his surcoat and realized Bledsoe also played the part of Sir Damian.

"I met you guys briefly this morning," Bledsoe continued, "but now it's time to take a whack at the most important aspect of the Middle Ages: fighting. Now, we've got a mixed crowd here. Some of you have never fought, some have a little experience, and a few of you are just about champion level. Kev Dyson here could probably demolish Sir Lancelot himself."

Bledsoe gestured toward a knight in the group with black armor and a panther emblem on his surcoat. He was around twenty, with dark hair and a serious set to his face. Kev showed no emotion, Frank noticed, as the other knights turned to look at him.

"Kev's been doing this since he was a kid," Bledsoe went on, "and he's about as good as they get. Anyway, we're going to start with the basics today. No matter how much you know, everyone pay attention. The point of the fighting is to kill each other—but to do it safely." A few of the knights chuckled.

"First let me tell you about your armor," Bledsoe said. "The body armor is made of high-grade plastic, unbreakable. This stuff could even stop a bullet. Don't laugh. A friend of mine tried it once."

Bledsoe reached down and picked up a cylindrical stick about a yard long that had a hilt at the base. "For swords we use these," Bledsoe explained. "They're made of rattan, which is a lot like bamboo, but heavier. You hold it like so and swing it like this." Holding the "sword" at the hilt, Bledsoe made a couple of wide-swinging slashes with the weapon.

"How hard can we hit?" Chet piped up.

"Only as hard as you can," Bledsoe said with a grin. "Come here."

Chet walked over to Bledsoe a little hesitantly. Bledsoe cocked back his sword and swung it full force into Chet's chest. *Thwack!* Chet staggered a step from the blow.

"Still there?" Bledsoe asked.

"Yeah," Chet answered, a bit stunned. "I mean, I felt it, but it didn't really hurt."

"That's the beauty. You can fight as hard as you want without anyone getting injured. Now try to hit me," Bledsoe said, handing Chet a sword from a pile of weapons on the ground.

Chet swung at Bledsoe, but at the last possible second Bledsoe lifted his sword and fended off the blow.

"Obviously when someone swings at you," Bledsoe explained, "you try to block the blow. And to help you, we've got these." Bledsoe picked up a round shield made of aluminum and slipped his arm through two rings in back. "You fit your arm into the shield on your weak side and use your strong arm for the sword."

"How do you kill someone?" a knight asked.

"Bloodthirsty, aren't we?" Bledsoe joked. "Okay, it works like this. If your opponent gets a good solid hit on one of your arms or legs, that arm or leg is wounded and you can't use it anymore. This means you might have to kneel down or drop your shield and fight with your weak arm. If your opponent gets a solid blow on your chest or head, you're dead. At least for that particular battle. And this all works on the honor system. Everyone clear?"

The knights all nodded. "All right, let's go for it," Bledsoe called. "Put on your helmets, pick up a sword and shield, then pair off with a partner."

After strapping on his helmet and getting his weaponry, Joe started moving toward Chet. But feeling someone tap him on the shoulder, Joe turned to find himself face-to-face with Kev Dyson. Realizing Dyson wanted to pair off with him, Joe wondered how he'd do against such an experienced fighter.

"Men of armor," Bledsoe commanded, "engage your foe in combat!"

At once most of the knights began swinging at

their partners, and the sounds of grunts and thwacks and clangs filled the air. Some of the bystanders began to cheer, and Jimmy waved his toy sword.

Joe stared into the eye slits on Dyson's visor, surprised at how heavy the shield and sword felt. Dyson chose to use no shield and merely stared back at Joe, holding his sword at the ready.

He's testing me, Joe thought, hearing his own breathing inside the helmet. He's waiting for me to show him what I've got. Okay, tough guy, I'll show you!

Suddenly Joe swung hard at Dyson's black helmet, but Dyson easily knocked the blow away with his sword. This guy's good, Joe thought.

Thwack! Dyson's sword crashed into Joe's left shoulder, sending shock vibrations all the way down Joe's arm. Joe realized his left arm was now out of commission, so he dropped his shield and faced Dyson again.

This time Dyson started circling around Joe, easy and graceful as the panther on his surcoat. Turning to keep facing Dyson, Joe gazed into his opponent's visor again. He knows I'm new at this so he's waiting for me to get mad, Joe thought, sweat trickling down his cheek. But I won't. I'll stay as cool as he is.

Suddenly Dyson slashed at Joe's left shoulder and Joe went to block, but it was a fake and Dyson wheeled his sword around with two hands and smashed Joe's weapon, sending it sailing away. Wow, Joe thought. He's fast!

Joe loped away a few steps to retrieve his sword. But as he reached down for the weapon Dyson thwacked Joe hard on the right leg! Isn't he supposed to give me a chance to get my sword? Joe wondered, feeling the stinging sensation run down his leg.

"That knight got his leg chopped off!" Jimmy cried out.

Joe picked up his sword and knelt on his "chopped-off" right leg, feeling foolish and angry. His hair was soaked with sweat, and his breathing sounded even louder inside the helmet. Dyson's laughing at me, Joe thought. He could have killed me right away, but instead he wants to take me apart piece by miserable piece.

Joe made a wild, desperate slash at Dyson's left leg. But Dyson's foot came slamming down on Joe's sword and then—*clang*—Joe heard his head ringing like a bell! His helmet echoed a blow he hadn't even seen, and the vibrations from it ran halfway down his body. Joe realized he was now officially dead.

Joe lay on the ground and watched Dyson walk away from him without a word. He's a champ at the sport, Joe thought, but certainly not at sportsmanship. Joe then turned his attention to the other fighters, only about half of them still alive and fighting.

Joe watched one knight send a ferocious blow straight down on another knight's helmet. Joe winced at the clanging noise, as the knight receiving the blow staggered backward, then toppled to the ground with a thud. The knight lay on the grass for a few moments.

Something's wrong, Joe realized. That guy isn't moving!

4 Slipping into the Mud

Joe jumped up, ran over to the fallen knight, and knelt beside him. He noticed that the knight's helmet was cracked down the middle in front. "Are you all right?" Joe asked, touching the knight's arm. The knight didn't move or reply.

"Hey, Steve," Joe called. "Over here!"

Steve Bledsoe instantly ran over to Joe and knelt beside him. Bledsoe shook the knight's shoulder. "Hey, you okay? Can you hear me?"

The knight still did not respond.

"What happened?" Bledsoe asked Joe.

"He took a blow on the head, and apparently it cracked his helmet," Joe answered.

"Let's get this thing off," Bledsoe said, undoing the knight's chin strap. He then very gently eased off the helmet and found a freshly bleeding cut at the top of the knight's forehead.

"Mommy, is the knight dead?" Jimmy's voice shook.

"No, he's not dead," the mother replied. "It's just pretend." She firmly guided her son away from the bloody sight.

By now the rest of the knights were gathering around the prone body. The knight who had delivered the blow was in front, his face ashen. Kev Dyson hung at the back of the crowd but seemed bored by the scene, Joe noticed. He saw Frank in the crowd, too.

"Hey, fella, can you hear me?" Bledsoe urged, shaking the knight's shoulder again. "Come on, we've got to talk to you here!"

There was silence. Then the knight moaned, and Joe saw him slowly open his eyes.

"Hey, welcome back," Bledsoe said, obviously relieved. "How're you feeling?"

The knight moaned again. "What's your name?" Bledsoe asked.

"Oh . . . uh . . ." the knight muttered, "it's, uh, uh . . . Daniel. I think."

"Daniel, buddy, you're gonna be just fine," Bledsoe said, encouraging him. "Just take it easy, and we'll get you out of here in no time."

Frank noticed Krause standing beside him, scribbling in a notepad. "Looks like there might be a story here after all," Krause said, still chewing his gum.

"Glad about that, aren't you?" Frank retorted. Then remembering he was also supposed to be a reporter, Frank pulled out a memo pad and pen, which he usually carried in his back pocket, and began scribbling, too.

Suddenly the knights began to clap and Frank saw Bledsoe helping Daniel to his feet. Bledsoe instructed another knight to help Daniel over to the first-aid station, promising to join them there soon.

"Okay," Bledsoe called to the knights, "you're free now, but be back here at three o'clock. And bring all your armor. I want to check everything again."

The knights quietly walked away, and Bledsoe began examining the split helmet. "I don't understand," Bledsoe confided to Joe. "This stuff is unbreakable, and I checked everything thoroughly this morning. This just shouldn't have happened."

"I'm sure it's not your fault," Joe assured him.

"Do me a favor," Bledsoe said, handing Joe the split helmet. "Take this to the costume trailer for me. And, please, don't let anyone else see it."

"Sure," Joe said. He began walking across the field with the helmet. In a moment Frank was walking beside him, but before either of them could speak, a strange character caught their eye.

A rather short man dressed in the tattered costume of a beggar approached them. His face was partially covered by a cloth mask similar to ones worn during times of plague.

"That fighting back there was pretty authentic," the beggar said to the Hardys. "I like it that way."

Before the Hardys could respond, the beggar walked away, limping slightly.

"Look," Joe said, turning back to Frank and passing him the helmet. "I'm pretty sure this wasn't an accident. If you look right above the split, you can see the helmet might have been scored with a blade."

"I think you're right," Frank said, studying the helmet. "And I wouldn't be surprised if this was done by the same person who rigged that stand to fall."

"Yep," Joe agreed, "and if Bledsoe checked the equipment early this morning like he says he did, this helmet must have been tampered with since then."

"Mr. Growtowski told me the stand was also put up this morning," Frank added.

"Which means that the dirty work was done sometime this morning before the fair opened at eleven," Joe figured. "The volunteers all got here around nine, and most of the fair staff got here earlier."

The Hardys soon found Growtowski in the mock village, talking to Jimmy's angry mother. "My child is terrified," she was saying. "This place is dangerous, and I want my money back. I bought a five-day pass, and I want every cent of it refunded!"

"I'm sorry you feel this way," Growtowski replied, "but I'll be happy to give you a refund." He then motioned to Carla, the girl Joe had met earlier, who was passing by. "Carla, would you be so kind as

31

to take this woman to the gate and make sure she gets a refund for her five-day pass?"

"Anything you say, Mr. Growtowski," Carla said.

As Carla led the mother and little boy away, Growtowski turned to Frank and Joe. "I suppose you want to talk to me about this second mishap," he said.

"Afraid so," Frank answered.

"Let's take a walk," Growtowski suggested.

The Hardys and Growtowski strolled away from the village as Frank and Joe began to explain the facts as far as they knew them.

"It seems unlikely," Frank said as the trio approached the field, "that the culprit was specifically trying to hurt that knight or hurt a certain girl. It was a whole group of girls who fell, and as of this morning the culprit couldn't have known who was going to be assigned each helmet. Which means the bad guy here is probably trying to hurt the fair or get to you personally."

"And we think this person is probably connected to the fair," Joe added. "Either a staff member or a volunteer. If anyone else had been messing around with stuff this morning they would have been noticed."

"I see," Growtowski said, frowning. "Well, there are forty-six staff members who travel with the fair. And then there are some fifty-odd volunteers who signed up for this location yesterday."

"Can you think of any suspicious behavior from any of these people?" Frank asked.

They walked a moment in silence, passing a

costumed man who was swallowing a fiery sword to the delight and astonishment of the onlookers. "Well, maybe one person," Growtowski finally said. "I'm speaking of the gentleman you met earlier— Alvin Sing."

"Tell us more," Joe urged.

"Sing controls the computer system, though a few others and I have access to it," Growtowski explained. "But he's also got a lot of new secret files in there. You need a password to get to them, and he's the only one who knows it. When we're on location, he likes to get to the trailer around dawn and work on those files a few hours before we open."

"Everyone likes a little privacy," Frank observed.

"True," Growtowski said. "But there's something else. One morning I came into the trailer earlier than usual, and I could see he was shutting down the files as fast as possible so I wouldn't see them. Afterward he acted nervous, and he's not the nervous type."

"Is that it?" Joe asked.

"That's it," Growtowski replied. "It's not much, I know, but I'm trying to be as helpful as I can."

"How long has Sing been with you?" Joe asked.

"Four years," Growtowski replied. "I've been running the fair for twelve years now, and he's the best general manager I've ever had."

The trio had entered a section of forest and began strolling through the shady foliage. "How did you get into this business?" Frank asked, hoping that the more he knew about the fair's history, the closer he'd get to the root of its problems.

33

"Well, the story goes back to my grandfather," Growtowski said with a fond smile. "He worked in a meat-packing plant in Cleveland, but he was an ambitious man, and after years of hard work he bought a few plants of his own. He got pretty rich, and he decided to buy himself one very extravagant thing."

"What was it?" Frank asked, genuinely curious.

"An authentic medieval sword," Growtowski answered. "It's funny. He wasn't especially interested in the Middle Ages, but nevertheless that sword became his most treasured possession."

"Interesting," Joe said.

"And he kept that sword even though his business started failing and he ended up losing the bulk of his money," Growtowski continued. "Then he passed the sword on to my father, who was, in fact, very interested in the Middle Ages."

"Probably because of the sword," Joe put in.

"That's right," Growtowski confirmed. "Anyway, when my father passed away, I inherited the sword and I've also inherited his interest in things medieval. So I started up this traveling fair."

"Where's the sword now?" Frank wanted to know.

"On loan to a museum," Growtowski answered. "I keep it in museums almost all of the time now."

Through the trees the lake was visible, and a few visitors sat by the shimmering water, eating picnic lunches. Far away, the singing of the troubador mixed with the sound of children laughing.

34

"I love this fair," Growtowski continued, gazing toward the water. "It's historical, it's exciting, and most of all it just gives folks a fun place to go and enjoy themselves."

"I hate to say this," Frank said, "but I think we should call in the police. They should know about these accidents."

"I suppose you're right," Growtowski said, "but . . ."

"But what?" Joe asked.

"Their presence will alarm people," Growtowski reasoned. "Let's keep them away. The police might even want me to shut down for a while until this whole thing is resolved."

"Well, it's better than someone else getting hurt, isn't it?" Joe remarked.

"Yes, of course it is," Growtowski agreed. "But then, you see, I may have to shut the fair down for good."

"Why?" Frank asked.

"Last year business was down," Growtowski explained, "and I went through most of my savings just to stay open. We travel all over the east coast, but this park is my first and best location of the season and I need a decent gate here to move on to the next spot. To put it bluntly, if I don't at least break even this week, I'll have to close Avalon down for the summer. And maybe forever."

As Growtowski continued gazing at the lake, Frank exchanged a look with Joe.

"I'll tell you what," Frank said to Growtowski.

"We'll hold off calling the cops and making a big production out of this. Meanwhile my brother and I will do everything we can to figure out who's sabotaging your fair."

"There's an advantage to that, too," Joe said. "If the police come in, chances are the accidents will stop for a while and the culprit won't be found. But then who knows when whoever it is will start up the dangerous games again? He could strike anytime. But maybe if Frank and I work undercover here, we can nail this guy once and for all."

"I can't thank you boys enough," Growtowski said, clearly touched. "Apparently chivalry isn't gone for good."

Growtowski and the Hardys made their way back to the mock village, stopping at an area where several sporting and game booths had been set up. A sign across the road announced Mudde Fights! Underneath the sign was a large pit filled with mud and surrounded by a low fence.

"It's about that time," the barker of the Mudde booth called. "You know what I mean. Time for another mud fight! Do I have any volunteers? Let's see. How about two lovely damsels this time?"

A large, dark-haired woman laughed and stepped forward to volunteer. A crowd was gathering near the booth, and the Hardys noticed Callie and Iola standing nearby.

"Go on," Iola urged Callie. "You haven't done anything fun all day. I think you deserve a fight in the mud."

36

"Iola," Callie protested, "I am not going to wrestle a stranger in a big vat of mud! No way!"

"We want Callie! We want Callie!" Frank and Joe began chanting as they walked over to the Mudde booth.

"Oh, come on, young lady," the barker called to Callie, "have a go. Who knows? You may end up as the fair's Queen of the Mudde!"

"All right, all right," Callie said, tossing up her hands. "I'll do it."

Callie and her opponent each zipped on a dark jumpsuit that the barker gave them and then stepped into the mud pit.

"Go for it, Susan!" someone shouted from the crowd. The large woman turned and waved. Then she and Callie moved around tentatively in the sloshy mud, which came about halfway up to their knees.

"All you have to do," the barker explained, "is pin your opponent down in the mud for a count of five. Understand?" Callie and Susan nodded. The barker then blew a little whistle, and the two adversaries began circling each other in the mud.

"This I've got to see," Frank confided to Joe. "She doesn't even like to spill a soft drink on her shirt."

Susan grabbed at Callie as the crowd began shouting, "Go, go, go, go!" With a burst of determination, Callie threw the large woman into the mud, but then Susan grabbed Callie's ankle and Callie slipped into the slimy mud herself.

37

The crowd went crazy as the two opponents wrestled and rolled in the goo, each trying to pin the other one down.

Then all of a sudden, there was a piercing scream. "Stop!" the barker called. But the mud was so slippery that the wrestlers had trouble holding still. Another shrill scream came. This time Frank recognized the voice immediately. It was Callie!

5 The Eagle's Eye

Frank leapt over the low fence into the mud pit and sloshed his way toward Callie.

"Frank," Callie cried, standing up, "I've got something sharp in my arm. Right below my shoulder." Her dark-haired opponent hovered nearby, obviously concerned.

"Don't move," Frank instructed the mud-covered woman. He examined the upper part of Callie's arm and found a large chunk of glass stuck through her jumpsuit. He also noticed dark blood mixing with the brown mud on Callie's sleeve.

"It's a piece of glass," Frank told her as he eased the shard out. "Okay, let's all be very careful," he cautioned as he, Callie, and Susan made their way out of the mud pit.

Callie's opponent quickly stepped out of her

jumpsuit and, after glaring at Growtowski, rejoined her family and stormed off.

Another unhappy customer, Frank thought. He showed the piece of glass to Joe, Growtowski, and the barker, and Joe immediately stepped into the pit and began carefully running his gloved hand through the mud. Growtowski escorted Callie to the all-too-familiar first-aid station.

"When was the last mud fight?" Frank asked the barker.

"About forty-five minutes ago," the barker answered, less merry than before. "I took a break for lunch."

"I assume there haven't been any other problems like this today?" Frank asked.

"No," the barker replied. "So far it's been all good clean fun. If you know what I mean."

Joe stepped out of the pit, the lower part of his arm and leg armor stained with mud, and showed Frank several more large chunks of glass. "You'd better check the pit thoroughly," Frank advised the barker. He then noticed Krause hurrying over to the pit.

"How do you suppose the glass got there?" Krause asked eagerly.

"We don't know," Joe said curtly. "Why don't you dust the mud for fingerprints."

"Funny," Krause replied, chewing his gum. "Very funny."

Frank and Joe quickly walked away from the Mudde booth. "It must be the work of the guy who wrecked the platform—the Knight of the Flaming Sword," Joe said.

"And he must have done it in the last forty-five minutes," Frank added. "That's when the last fight was."

"The problem is," Joe said, "he could have done it without anyone noticing what he was doing. All he had to do was toss some glass into the pit."

"So this mystery remains clear as mud," Frank said, kicking dirt with his foot.

The day passed without further incident and around closing time, at seven, after Joe changed out of his armor, the Hardys had a final conference with Growtowski.

"I'm going to stay in the park tonight instead of my motel room," Growtowski told the Hardys. "I'll catch a few hours' sleep on the couch in the trailer and spend the rest of the time on the alert for anything fishy." Growtowski handed Frank a piece of paper. "Here's the trailer phone number if you need me."

In the parking lot the Hardys said goodbye to Callie and Iola, both bandaged now, and drove off in their van with Chet. They soon stopped at a diner a short way down the highway from the fair.

"I'll be back," Joe said as Frank and Chet took a booth by the window. Frank noticed some familiar faces at a table across the room and realized it was the troubadour, the Juggler, and the Enchantress in their regular clothes. Frank nodded in their direction, and they waved back.

41

"I called Phil," Joe reported as he took a seat at the booth, referring to their friend Phil Cohen, who often helped them on their cases. "I gave him the phone number for Growtowski's trailer, and he said there was a pretty good chance he could tap into Sing's secret computer files by modem."

"If anyone can do it, it's Phil," Frank remarked. "He's a genius when it comes to computers."

"So who do you think the saboteur is?" Chet wondered, eager to solve the new case.

"I say it's Kev Dyson," Joe stated.

"Why?" Frank asked.

A waitress brought sodas to the table, and the boys paused until she left. "Because the guy's mean," Joe answered, gripping his glass. "I should know. He killed me today."

"Oh, great detective work," Frank challenged. "No motive, no evidence. Just a feeling the guy is mean."

"All right, Sherlock," Joe countered, "what sort of a motive have you put together?"

"So far the best thing I can think of," Frank said, "is that somebody wants to destroy the fair because it's competition."

"Who would that be?" Chet questioned.

"Well, Sing, for one," Frank offered. "He's been the general manager of Avalon for a few years, and he knows the business. Maybe he wants to start up his own fair."

"And you've got a whole truckload of evidence to prove that, of course," Joe scoffed.

"You got me there," Frank admitted. "The fact is, we've got nothing so far but a bunch of dangerous accidents and a note from someone claiming to be the Knight of the Flaming Sword. We think it's someone connected to the fair, but we're not even sure about that."

"Tomorrow we're going to have to be sharp," Joe said thoughtfully. "We're going to have to get some real clues. I just hope nothing serious—"

Frank cut him off with a shudder. "Me too, little brother. Me too."

The next morning Frank and Joe entered the kitchen to find their aunt Gertrude setting out plates of bacon and eggs. The Hardys' parents were out of town, and Aunt Gertrude was currently in charge of the house.

"How was the fair yesterday?" Aunt Gertrude asked, pouring orange juice into glasses.

"Oh, *fairly* exciting," Joe joked, not wanting to worry his aunt.

After Aunt Gertrude left the room, Frank handed Joe the day's edition of the *Bayport Star*. The paper was opened to the middle of the first section, and Joe's eyes jumped to the headline: Danger at the Medieval Fair.

"Just as we feared," Joe said, scanning the page. "The article speculates these weren't just accidents at the fair." Frank then turned the paper over, and on the next page Joe saw a large advertisement for the fair offering free use of costumes for the day.

43

"I told Mr. Growtowski about the reporter," Frank mentioned. "He must have decided to send this in soon afterward."

"Well, even the *Bayport Star* is engaged in battle," Joe said, tossing the paper onto the table.

The Hardys finished their breakfast quickly and arrived at the fair a half hour before opening. Frank went to confer with Growtowski while Joe carried a duffel bag containing his armor through a side door into the castle.

Joe entered the locker room on the ground floor and spotted Chet and Iola retrieving their costumes from their assigned lockers. "Check your armor," Joe warned Chet. "I took mine home yesterday just to be on the safe side."

"You know," Iola said, smoothing her pink gown on its hanger, "I'm starting to realize you guys have the better job here. All I do is stand around and look pretty while you knights get to yell and fight and do all the fun stuff."

"Sorry," Chet said, pulling out his helmet. "Girls weren't knights."

"This fair's not fair!" Iola retorted, smiling at her wordplay. She then noticed Carla getting her costume out of a nearby locker. "Hey, Carla," Iola called, "have there ever been any girl knights at Avalon?"

Carla slowly turned to Iola. "Uh, no," she answered. "Mr. Growtowski won't allow it. He says it's not historically accurate."

"Well, then, I guess we'd better stick to the

script," Iola said. "Come on, serving girl," she said playfully, "help me with my crown."

Carla looked startled but walked over to help Iola.

"Hey, I could get used to this," Iola joked as Carla adjusted the crown.

"Yes, m'lady," Carla said.

Joe watched the shy girl leave, carrying her costume. "I don't know if she realized you were joking," he said. Iola shrugged and went off to change.

"C'mon," Chet urged. "We don't want to be late."

"I'll be there in a sec," Joe called as Chet headed off to the men's changing room. Joe then made his way toward Kev Dyson, who was now turning the combination on his locker.

"Hey, Kev," Joe said as Dyson started pulling a large canvas bag out of his locker. "It was a real experience fighting with you yesterday."

"Thanks," Dyson muttered, barely acknowledging Joe.

"You know what your problem is?" Joe remarked.

Dyson turned to look at Joe.

"You were born about five centuries too late," Joe continued. "I mean, watching you out there in the armor, I felt like you should have lived back in the Middle Ages. You should have been a real knight. That's how good you are."

"I'm glad you see that," Dyson said. "Most of these guys are just out there clowning around, swinging sticks and cracking jokes. But there's a lot more to it. Believe me, knighthood goes pretty deep."

"For someone like you," Joe commented, "this fair must seem downright stupid."

"I come here because I like the sport of fighting," Dyson said, shutting his locker. "But the truth is, I find it worse than stupid. I find it insulting. I'm only saying this to you because I think you might understand."

"I do," Joe assured him.

"All you other knights go by a bunch of fake names," Dyson continued. "One guy even calls himself Sir Harry of Gorilla-ville. But I take the name Sir Geoffrey of Martel, a real knight from the twelfth century. I try to do things as he would." Dyson apparently had forgotten something in his locker because he began turning the combination again.

"Tell me about Sir Geoffrey," Joe said, secretly watching Dyson's hands.

"On second thought," Dyson said, opening the locker and pulling a pair of orange armbands from it, "I'd rather not. You're the enemy." Dyson shut the locker, then walked off toward the changing room with his bag.

After Joe had strapped on all the various parts of his armor, he left the castle and headed for the field. Just as he was realizing how sore both his arms were from wielding the weaponry, Frank trotted over.

"Growtowski said things were calm here," Frank reported. "Let's hope they stay that way."

"I spoke to Dyson," Joe said. "He takes this medieval stuff really seriously. And he doesn't think anyone else takes it seriously enough. He told me he based his character on a real knight named Sir Geoffrey of Martel. I think there may be something to it. When you get a chance later, could you hit the library and see if there's anything on this guy?"

"It's worth a try," Frank said. "I'll see you later."

Joe continued to the center of the field, where the knights were gathering for another training session. Frank met up with Callie, and as they strolled the grounds, he told her about the Knight of the Flaming Sword.

"Looks like another good crowd today," Callie commented as they passed by the castle. "I guess that ad helped offset the newspaper article."

"There's a long line at the costume tent," Frank noted. "Of course, that's because there's no rental fee today."

As they entered the mock village, Callie asked, "So where do you think the mystery knight will strike next?"

"I've been wondering the same thing," Frank said, scanning the area.

"That looks pretty safe," Callie said, glancing at a loud puppet show where a group of kids were gathered.

"What about that?" Frank asked, looking at the

47

Drench a Wench booth, where Carla sat on a platform suspended over a pool of water. Suddenly a beanbag hit the target and—splash—Carla dropped into the drink!

"Well, it doesn't look too fun," Callie said sympathetically as Carla glumly pulled herself out of the pool, "but at least water's better than glass."

Two hours later Callie went off to find Iola, and Frank met Joe in the field. A crowd was gathered around a woman in hunting clothes with a thick leather glove on her left hand. Beside the woman were three blocks of wood, and a large hunting bird perched on each block.

"Good afternoon, ladies and gentlemen," the woman addressed the crowd. "I am Martina, the master falconer. Falconry, you know, was very popular in the Middle Ages. By falconry, I mean the sport of hunting with falcons, hawks, and, for the very daring, eagles."

"Stay alert," Joe whispered to Frank. "Those birds could be dangerous."

The falconer proceeded to prove Joe's point by having the falcon and hawk attack a lure that, when swung by a string, resembled a small bird.

"Now, if you folks are game, we'll take a look at the golden eagle," Martina told the crowd. She then untethered the third bird from its block and removed the leather hood from its head, and the bird stepped up onto her glove.

The eagle was twice as large as the other birds, and its fierce, dark eyes slowly scanned the faces of the crowd. The talons and beak appeared to be extremely sharp, Joe noticed.

"Oooh, look at that big bird," cried a little girl in a pink dress.

The falconer lifted her glove, and the eagle flew into the air. Once the bird was above tree level, it began sailing in stunning arcs across the sky, its wingspan amazingly large. Every head in the crowd craned upward, gazing at the awesome creature in flight.

Then suddenly the eagle slowed, hovering a moment in midair. The eagle turned its head, and it seemed to Joe that its fierce eyes were aimed directly at him. Then, with frightening speed, the eagle began diving straight for Joe's head!

6 Vengeance

Joe glimpsed the eagle's sharp talons as he quickly turned his head and felt the wings flap past his face. He saw the eagle chasing a small brown rabbit that was scampering madly across the grass. People around Joe were rushing to clear out of the bird's path.

"Where'd the rabbit come from?" Joe yelled, his heart pounding.

The rabbit was zigzagging crazily, trying to flee the eagle, which was flying after it very close to the ground. With a mean squawk, the eagle brushed past a man. "Ow!" the man yelled. "It scratched me!" A woman dove to the ground when she saw the eagle flying straight for her.

"Everyone stay calm!" the falconer called to the crowd. "The eagle just wants the rabbit! It will only hurt you if you get in the way!"

But the little girl in pink who was so awed by the eagle was now even more fascinated by the rabbit. "Look, it's Peter Cottontail!" the girl cried in delight. She began chasing after the rabbit.

Frank then saw the eagle slow its wings and focus its gaze on the playful girl. Frank realized the eagle saw the girl as competition for its prey.

"Fall to the ground!" Frank yelled across the field. "Little girl, fall to the ground!"

But the girl kept chasing the rabbit, and the eagle went after her. Faster, faster, the eagle flew. Frank started running toward the girl.

The eagle began diving for the girl, its talons out, sharp as daggers. Doubling his speed, Frank rushed in front of the eagle's path, frantically waving his arms.

Frank felt a sharp slash on his forearm, heard a woosh of feathers, and saw the eagle lift into the air. Then Frank saw a net come slamming down on top of the rabbit. The falconer quickly handed the net to a staff member who carried the rabbit away.

"'Bye, 'bye, Peter!" The little girl in pink waved to the disappearing rabbit.

"Nice save," Joe said, running over to Frank.

"I was just waiting for my turn to get injured," Frank said, touching the blood on his arm.

Soon the falconer returned the eagle to its perch and Growtowski, his face red, his hair wild, came running up. "It's all right!" he called to the scattering crowd. "The eagle has been caught! If you'd like to head over to the village, free refreshments will be served! Please, I'd like you all to have some free refreshments!"

The Hardys heard a woman exclaim, "That was the most frightening thing I ever saw in my life! I am going to demand a full refund."

"So am I," a man agreed. "I came here for some fun, not to be attacked by a predatory bird!"

Frank and Joe ran to Growtowski, passing Krause on the field. Krause was no longer wearing the monk's robe, but he was scribbling away on his pad.

"That rabbit would never have come out with so many people around," Growtowski fumed to the Hardys. "Someone deliberately brought it here and let it loose!"

"The problem is," Frank pointed out, "someone could have released the rabbit and not been seen."

"This guy is slippery," Joe said, angrily glancing around. "But who is he?"

Just then Martina, the falconer, came trotting over. "I found this attached to the eagle's perch," she said, handing a piece of parchment to Growtowski. The Hardys read it over Growtowski's shoulder. The message was similar to the one the Hardys had found the day before:

Though you may think you're here for fun this week,
My sword is sharper than the eagle's beak.
   —The Knight of the Flaming Sword

"What's that?" Krause asked, running up to the group. But before Krause could get a good look at the note, Frank snatched it from Growtowski's hand and slipped it into his back pocket.

"What's what?" Frank replied.

"Look, I know you guys are reporters for your school newspaper and all," Krause said, his annoyance growing. "But there's a real story going on here, and the public has a right to know about it. In a real newspaper, not just from some high school amateurs!"

"There's nothing for them to know," Joe insisted.

"I'm going to the library," Frank told Joe. He headed for the parking lot, Krause badgering him along the way.

After unsuccessfully trying to find someone who had seen the rabbit released, Joe found Chet by the Foode and Drinke booth, gnawing on a thick sausage. "I guess you're dripping grease onto your armor on purpose," Joe teased his friend. "That way the enemy blows will just slide off, right?"

Before Chet could counter the jest, a clamorous din was heard and Sir Damian's men charged into the village, wildly banging their swords on their shields.

"It's a raid, it's a raid!" Chet yelled, frantically tossing his sausage into the air. As the outlaw knights began knocking things over and shouting threats, Chet grabbed for his sword, but in his excitement he knocked the weapon into a pickle barrel.

Joe laughed out loud. Then he caught a glimpse

of Dyson slashing at a foe with controlled fury. With Dyson busy, Joe saw his chance and instantly turned and ran for the castle.

Joe pushed through the side door into the locker room. It was empty, so he went straight to Dyson's locker and turned the combination from memory. Joe opened the locker and noticed a book resting on the upper shelf.

Glancing around to make sure he was still alone, Joe took the book down. It was *The Art of the Knight*. Joe leafed through the pages, stopping at a chapter titled Falconry. He turned the pages, finding information on falcons, hawks, and eagles, accompanied by detailed illustrations. Then Joe noticed a piece of paper stuck inside the book near the end of the chapter. This could be important, he thought, but I need to get out of here. He read the note quickly and then stuck it into his pocket.

A while later, in the Bayport library, Frank was turning pages in a dusty old volume devoted to real knights of the Middle Ages. He leafed through information on the Crusades, the jousting tournaments, and the training of the knights. Then he found the section on the French knight Sir Geoffrey of Martel. He quickly became engrossed in the material.

With a loud noise a book fell to the floor from a nearby shelf. Startled, Frank glanced up and saw a long sword slide menacingly through from the other side of the shelf.

"Who's there?" Frank called.

No answer. Frank rose and slowly moved toward the sword. He pulled a few books from the shelf—and saw Chet, back in regular clothes, grinning at him from the other side.

"*En garde*," Chet joked.

"What are you doing here?" Frank asked, anger mixed with amusement. "And what are you doing?"

"This is a prop sword from the fair," Chet said, pulling out the sword and knocking a few more books to the floor. "I couldn't resist. But I do have a message for you."

"What?" Frank asked impatiently.

"Joe found a note in Dyson's locker," Chet said, suddenly serious. "The note said 'Meet me at the filling station right off Exit twenty-nine on the highway at five o'clock sharp.' Joe thinks we ought to stake out the place, and he wanted you to be there. It's four now so we'd better get moving."

"Let's go," Frank said, returning the fallen books to the shelf.

Frank and Chet picked up Joe at the fair, and soon they were cruising down the highway in the Hardy van. "Sir Geoffrey of Martel was a real knight," Frank explained as he drove. "He fought with great honor in the Crusades, but by the time he returned home, he'd completely lost his mind. He took a vow of vengeance against the world and traveled across the French countryside, killing innocent people."

"Sort of like his own personal crusade," Joe observed.

"Yeah, and maybe Kev Dyson's doing the same thing," Chet chimed in, sitting between the two brothers. "He hates anything about the fair that isn't absolutely accurate. This really points a finger at him, doesn't it?"

"And here's another finger," Joe said. "The note I found about tonight's meeting was stuck in a book he had—in a chapter on falconry."

"So he might know something about getting an eagle to go berserk," Frank added.

"That's right," Joe responded. "I wonder what this mysterious meeting is all about."

"We'll soon find out," Frank said, steering the van off the highway at Exit 29.

"Look, there he is," Joe said as the van drove down the service road. Dyson was leaning against a red car beside a filling station.

"We can do sentry detail here," Frank said, pulling into a car-wash place just past the filling station.

"Five till five," Chet said, checking his watch.

Joe was already focusing a pair of small but high-powered binoculars on his target. Dyson came into view, calmly tapping his fingers against the car's door. "Cool as a cucumber," Joe noted.

"A lot of crazy people are," Chet said.

Precisely at five o'clock, a brown Camaro pulled into the filling station and parked a few feet ahead of Dyson's car on the side away from the Hardys. Dyson immediately went to the Camaro's window.

"Dyson's in the way," Joe said, peering through the binoculars. "Can't see the driver's face."

"What's going on?" Frank asked.

"Dyson's just talking to the driver," Joe answered.

"Does he look crazy, too?" Chet wondered.

"Not as crazy as you," Frank said, remembering the sword in the library.

"Wait," Joe said after a few minutes. "The driver just handed Dyson an envelope."

"A payoff!" Chet exclaimed.

The Camaro began backing out. Joe followed the car with the binoculars like a hawk tracking its prey. "It's a man, and he's wearing aviator sunglasses," Joe observed, "but I can't make out the face from here."

The Camaro began driving up the service road, and Frank was already maneuvering the van onto the road to follow. "I'll try to get close enough for us to get a look at the face," Frank said.

"I got the plates," Joe said, writing on a notepad.

The Camaro accelerated up the ramp onto the highway, and the Hardys' van soon followed. Traffic had thickened, and cars were now zooming by in every lane.

"Careful," Joe warned. "It's rush hour."

Frank kept close to the Camaro, waiting for a chance to drive up alongside it, but suddenly the Camaro switched lanes and started picking up speed.

"I think he knows we're following," Frank said, checking his rearview mirror and switching lanes.

"And he's driving like he's crazy," Chet announced.

Frank gunned the van, closing in fast on the Camaro. Seeing an opening, Frank started switching lanes to overtake the Camaro, but suddenly another car swerved into the new lane. Frank jerked the wheel to avoid collision. Instantly brakes squealed behind the van, followed by a cacophony of car horns. The Camaro sped away.

"Sorry," Frank apologized, "but it would have been an accident for sure."

"Rats!" Chet exclaimed, slapping his knee.

The Hardys arrived at the fair an hour before closing and went to Growtowski's trailer. Joe immediately called his friend on the Bayport police force, Con Riley, to have him trace the Camaro license plates.

"There's been another incident," Growtowski told Frank. "The blade came flying off the ax-thrower's ax. No one was hurt, but I sure would like to put a stop to this dangerous business."

"So would we," Frank agreed. "And we will."

After dinner with Chet, Iola, and Callie, Frank and Joe drove home. "This knight is getting to me," Joe complained as he stared out the van window into the night. "He really is."

"Take it easy," Frank said. "Mr. Growtowski says he still broke even today. No one's been badly hurt yet, and we've got a few leads to follow."

"So do you think the envelope held some sort of payoff?" Joe asked. "That could tie in with your theory about someone being in competition with the fair."

Frank steered the van onto the gravel driveway of the Hardys' home on Elm Street. "That's right," Frank said, parking the van. "We may be closer to this than we think."

The Hardys found their house quiet. Aunt Gertrude was apparently already asleep, and they carefully climbed the staircase, not wanting to wake her. Suddenly Frank stopped and motioned to Joe to keep still. "I thought I heard footsteps up in the study," he whispered.

"And Aunt Gertrude wouldn't be in there," Joe whispered back.

"I don't like this," Frank said, cautiously taking another step.

On the second floor, the Hardys quietly moved down the hallway and came to the study door. They paused for a moment, listening. Joe shrugged his shoulders. "I guess we—" He was cut off by the sound of a thud inside the room!

7 A Bloody Warning

Frank threw open the study door, but the room seemed to be empty. Joe raced through the dark-ned room to an open window.

"Someone's running down there!" Joe exclaimed, climbing out the window. "I'm going after him!"

Looking out the window, Frank saw a figure in a monk's robe with the hood up racing across the backyard. Joe jumped from the porch roof down to the lawn and began chasing after the figure.

The monk pushed through hedges into a neighboring backyard. Joe chased after him, keeping his eyes on the fleeing figure. Suddenly Joe tripped on a sprinkler and fell, slamming into the grass.

He sprang up and kept chasing the monk, who was farther away now, having jumped over a fence and run down a nearby street. But by the time Joe reached the street, the monk was gone.

Joe glanced up and down the block and heard a car engine start up. Joe peered hard into the dark, trying to make out who was inside the car.

Then the headlights flashed on, blinding Joe, and the car lunged straight at him. Joe leapt out of the way, then turned to see the car disappearing down the deserted street.

Moments later Frank ran up to Joe. "I came around to cut him off," Frank panted, "but I guess he got away."

"Sure did," Joe said, blinking his eyes. "That's twice we've lost someone today, and I don't like it!"

"He had on a monk's robe like the one Krause has been wearing," Frank noted, "but I guess the fair's got plenty of those."

"Yeah," Joe huffed, "and apparently they rent them out for after-hours break-ins!"

When Frank and Joe returned home, Joe flipped on the lights in the study, hoping to find some kind of clue, but other than an open drawer, nothing was out of place. Joe could still hear Aunt Gertrude breathing evenly in her room.

"Joe, come here!" Frank called in a loud whisper from across the hall.

Joe dashed into the boys' bedroom and stopped dead when he saw a dagger stuck into the headboard of Frank's bed. A glove was skewered on the dagger, and a liquid resembling blood was dripping from the glove onto Frank's pillow. There was a note on the pillow, the lettering similar to that in the other messages. The message read:

If you don't stop searching through the mud,
My sword will turn your flesh to blood.

Joe stared at the bloody warning a moment, then pulled the dagger and glove from the headboard. "We may not be getting any closer to this knight," Joe remarked, his anger returning, "but he sure is getting closer to us."

"Easy," Frank said, absorbed in thought. "We'll get him."

Joe reached inside the glove and pulled out a sponge soaked with a deep red liquid. "Fake blood," Joe announced. "The kind they carry at most novelty shops." Joe tossed the sponge and glove into a trash can, then went to the bathroom and returned, wiping his hands on a towel. "So why do you think he came here?" Joe asked.

"He knew we were following him this afternoon," Frank said, "and he wanted to scare us away."

"You know what's odd about this message?" Joe said, picking up the note.

"It's not signed 'The Knight of the Flaming Sword,'" Frank answered.

"Right," Joe replied. "What do you make of that?"

"I don't know yet," Frank said as he began pulling the bloody pillowcase off the pillow. "Maybe nothing."

"So what do we do now?" Joe asked.

"Let's wash this stuff in the sink," Frank said, stepping into the bathroom.

"Why not the laundry?" Joe wondered aloud.

"Because I don't want Aunt Gertrude having a heart attack," Frank said with a significant look.

"Good point," Joe said.

Soon Frank and Joe were in bed. Joe immediately fell asleep, but Frank's thoughts lingered on the mysterious monk for a while before he also drifted off to sleep.

While eating breakfast the next morning, Frank and Joe scanned the paper. They soon found an article with the headline "Danger at the Fair Continues."

"The hot-shot reporter strikes again," Joe sneered as he read the article. He flipped through the paper and found another advertisement for Avalon. He passed the page over to Frank.

"Now Growtowski's offering a special low rate for the banquet this evening," Frank commented.

"It seems there are some awfully dangerous things going on at this fair," Aunt Gertrude said, sipping a cup of tea across the table. "I hope you boys aren't getting mixed up in any of this.

Frank and Joe both took a spoonful of oatmeal.

"Are you getting mixed up in any of this?" Aunt Gertrude persisted.

"Oh, we've got a hand in solving things," Joe said. "But it's nothing to worry about. Honestly."

"I sincerely hope not," Aunt Gertrude said as she cleared her dishes and headed for the den.

Just then there was a knock at the back door. "I'll get it," Frank said, jumping up. After peering through the curtain window, Frank opened the door, and Phil Cohen, the Hardys' friend and technical expert, entered.

"I tapped into the fair's computer system," Phil said, tossing a stack of papers onto the table. "This is the bulk of what's in there, but I wasn't able to break into the secret files. Whoever created those files really wants to keep them secret."

"Is there any way to get to them?" Frank asked.

"If I can actually get on their computer," Phil explained, "there's a decent chance I can break the password. But I need to get inside the trailer and I need at least a half hour to work."

"Well, Sing can't be there all day," Joe said.

"But he could walk in at any time," Frank argued. "And if he found us there, it will surely cause some bad blood."

"Well, we might see some *real blood* if we don't get in there!" Joe protested.

"Tonight there's a banquet inside the castle," Frank said. "In the middle of the banquet, let's get into the trailer with Phil."

"Sounds plausible," Phil said. "What time should I be there?"

"The banquet starts at seven," Frank replied. "Meet us at the front gate at seven-thirty."

"I'll be there," Phil said. "There's not a computer geek in the county who can electronically outwit Phil Cohen. I'll see you brave chevaliers tonight." He gave an elaborate bow and let himself out the back door.

Just then the phone rang and Joe ran to the hall to answer it. Frank began leafing through the computer printout, which consisted mostly of ordinary information—payroll records, tax information, and advertising layouts. The only puzzling file was one called Chauvency, which merely listed names, dates, and phone numbers.

"That was Con Riley," Joe said, returning to the kitchen. "He says the Camaro is owned by someone named Marcia Segal. I called her home number but got a machine. We can try later, and I guess we should ask Mr. Growtowski if he knows her."

Listening to the radio as they drove back out to the fair, the Hardys heard several commercials for Avalon. "Mr. Growtowski's pouring some bucks into his advertising," Joe remarked.

"Well, those newspaper articles are pretty damaging," Frank said, steering the van. "He needs to do something to keep people coming."

"Fewer cars than yesterday," Joe commented as the van pulled into the fair's parking lot.

"And I don't see a brown Camaro anywhere," Frank noted.

After his morning fight practice, Joe met Frank on the field to watch the horse show. Bledsoe and Carla, dressed in the flowing robes and turbans of Turkish nobility, began performing a series of impressive stunts on the two Avalon horses.

"I just hope no one spooks the horses," Joe said

as he watched the horses strut across the field toward each other in a marching rhythm.

"That could be a real disaster," Frank agreed.

Soon several high wooden fences were brought out, and Carla maneuvered the chestnut horse about the field, jumping the steed over the fences in breathtaking leaps.

"She's some rider," Frank said, noticing a fierce look of determination on Carla's face.

"Man, you'd never guess it," Joe commented as Carla made a perfect landing. "She's so tame in real life."

"People love horses," Growtowski said, coming up behind the Hardys. "Matter of fact, I just hired some professional jousters to come out here on Sunday. They're from a group called Champions that Steve Bledsoe used to work with."

"You mean they charge each other on horseback with lances?" Joe asked eagerly.

"Just like the knights of yore," Growtowski said, smiling. "It's costing me an arm and a leg, but with proper advertising it could bring in a great crowd."

As Bledsoe and Carla finished their exhibition to a great round of applause, Frank turned to Joe. "Why don't you keep an eye on the archery demonstration. I'll check out the play across the field. Something's coming, I can feel it."

"Got it," Joe said, trotting away.

Frank soon came to a crowd gathered around a large wooden platform on wheels, where a medieval play was being performed. Actors dressed in period costumes as a butcher, a baker, and a fish-wife were comically arguing with each other in loud voices.

"My bread is the finest in the land!" the baker boasted.

"And thy prices the highest!" the fishwife screamed, slapping the baker with a large prop fish. The audience laughed at the gag.

"Hey, there," Callie called, approaching Frank. "I thought I'd catch the play." She followed his gaze. "What are you looking at?"

"The sun," Frank said, gesturing toward a wood-en "sun" with sharp rays that was now being raised over the stage by a rope on a pulley. "I'm on the lookout for trouble."

"Oh, yeah," Callie said, shielding her eyes. "I can barely see it because the real sun is so bright."

Frank looked back at the stage. "Check him out," he said. An actor dressed in a black robe with a hood shadowing his face had just appeared on-stage. He was carrying a long scythe.

"I wonder how many of those robes they've got here," Frank whispered. "I saw one just like it last night."

"That's the character of Death," Callie explained. "If he gets you with his scythe, well . . ." She smiled as she slid an ominous finger across her throat. "He was a character in a lot of medieval plays."

"And who shall I take next?" Death intoned as he threatened the other actors with his scythe.

67

"You. . . or you . . . or you?" Death then turned to the audience and called out, "Or maybe you!" He swung his scythe menacingly toward the crowd.

"Frank, look!" Callie cried, suddenly pointing up. Frank gazed into the glare of the real sun and saw what she meant. The prop sun with the sharp rays was now dangling by a thread, about to fall, and the butcher was standing right beneath it!

8 Inside the Mind of the Wizard

Frank dashed forward, leapt onto the stage, and shoved the butcher out of the way. The next second the sun came crashing down, one of its rays breaking off as it hit the stage.

After the initial shock, there was scattered applause from the audience, which Frank realized was for him. Embarrassed, he nodded to the crowd, then stepped down from the platform.

"I always knew you had star quality," Callie said, still applauding as Frank approached her.

As the actors bravely continued the performance, Frank looked up at the severed pulley. "Someone could have cut that rope halfway through in a few moments," Frank said, his frustration mounting. "These stunts are so devious, they're almost impossible to stop!"

"Nice show, huh?" a voice in the audience commented. Frank and Callie turned to see the tattered beggar whom the Hardys had seen the first day of the fair. Again the beggar's face was partially covered by a mask. "I've always been a fan of high drama," the beggar told Frank, and then he limped away.

"Who's that?" Callie wondered.

"I have no idea," Frank said, "but he seems to pop up at the oddest times—like whenever there's trouble. Why don't you tag after him and see if he leads to anything."

"Oh, thanks," Callie said, setting off to follow the beggar. "Give me the creepy ones to watch."

Frank then saw a familiar figure approaching. "I was across the way, counting on something to happen at the archery demonstration," Krause called, trotting up to Frank, "but you never know where this guy'll strike. He's pretty slick, isn't he?"

"I don't know who you're talking about," Frank answered.

"Oh, come on," Krause persisted, "we both know something funny is going on here, and I think you know more about it than I do. Now, in the name of good journalism, I wish you would share your information with me."

"Sorry, I'm just an amateur," Frank snapped, walking away.

"What's the matter?" Krause called after Frank. "Didn't get enough sleep last night?"

Now, there's an interesting comment, Frank thought, wondering if Krause was connected to the bloody glove and the message on his pillow. He went to join Joe at the archery demonstration. As Frank approached his brother, a man dressed as Robin Hood was loading an arrow into a large bow.

"How's this theory?" Frank asked Joe. "Krause is causing the accidents just so he'll have a good story to write about."

"Sure, it's possible," Joe said, watching the archer pull back the taut string of the bow. "But Krause's articles aren't exactly Pulitzer Prize material. I can't see why he'd risk some serious jail time to get them."

"Yeah, guess you're right," Frank said, wearily rubbing his eyes.

"Hey, don't feel bad," Joe said, turning to his brother. "I was starting to wonder if Bledsoe was doing this just to get a job for his jousting buddies—which is even flimsier than your Krause theory."

Just then Robin Hood sent his arrow thwanging into the center of a stuffed target. "That's what *we* need," Frank remarked. "A bull's-eye!"

By the time the medieval banquet began at seven, there were no new incidents or new clues. While some of the castle was equipped with modern facilities, like the locker room, most of the castle was designed to resemble the real thing, and such was the case with the Great Hall.

"Castles always had a great hall," Chet explained as he held court at a table with Frank, Joe, Callie, and Iola. "That's where the festivities were held. And, more important, where the food was served."

As the crowd enjoyed their appetizers, the troubadour and Juggler wandered about the hall entertaining the large gathering of chattering guests. Frank noticed Alvin Sing at a nearby table.

"Aren't those dangerous?" Joe asked, pointing to a massive wooden chandelier with wax candles, which hung from the high, vaulted ceiling.

"You bet," Chet answered. "Castles caught fire all the time. In fact, see those holes in the ceiling? They are there for pouring water through to douse the fires. Apparently some rich guy built this place and he wanted everything to be as authentic as possible."

"Boy, some people really get into this medieval act," Callie observed. "Today Frank had me follow this crazy beggar all over the fair. Then I ran into Mr. Growtowski, and he told me the guy comes every year and always tries to buy some sword Mr. Growtowski owns. It's like some people wish the Middle Ages were still going on."

"Could you pass the salt, sis?" Chet asked Iola.

"Don't call me 'sis,' knave," Iola proclaimed with mock seriousness. "My name is Princess Rowena."

The group laughed as Carla came to their table and refilled their tankards with iced tea. Frank and Joe appeared to be enjoying themselves, but in fact they were carefully watching every movement in the room.

"Thanks," Joe said as Carla refilled his tankard.

"You're welcome, sir," she said, blushing.

"My glass isn't quite full," Iola said imperiously.

She held out the tankard to Carla, who filled it another inch.

Suddenly three loud knocks were heard at the double doors that led from the kitchen. "I hope I'm not interrupting anything!" Sir Damian bellowed as he burst through the doors into the hall.

King Bertram rose from his table on a raised platform. "Yesterday you attacked innocent villagers," the king called back. "Now are you so cowardly as to attack us at supper?"

"Who are you calling cowardly?" Sir Damian countered, striding into the room. His band of knights marched through the double doors, each in full armor with weapons drawn. Dyson was there in his black armor, contempt etched on his face. Joe wondered just how far the guy would go in the interest of accuracy.

"I beseech you," King Bertram urged, "to attack us tomorrow when we are fully prepared. For now I graciously invite you to join us at the table."

"What are you serving?" Sir Damian asked playfully.

"Chicken," King Bertram replied.

"Then perhaps we should kill the chickens first," Sir Damian bantered. "And perhaps you should be the first one slaughtered!" Sir Damian's men laughed and banged their swords noisily on the tables.

Frank glanced at his watch and whispered to Joe; then he and Callie got up and started moving for the exit door.

"And where are you going?" Sir Damian called to Frank and Callie.

"We wish to escape the bloodshed," Frank replied, putting an arm around Callie. There was general laughter around the room as Frank and Callie left the hall.

As arranged, Frank and Callie met Phil by the front gate and walked him through the park toward the trailers. The park was mostly dark now, the only sign of life coming from the blazing windows of the castle.

When they came to the office trailer, Frank stuck a long metal device into the cylinder on the door and twisted it a few times, and the door opened.

"I'll help Phil get set up inside," Frank told Callie. "If you see anyone coming, give a knock at the door and play it casual."

Frank and Phil stepped inside the trailer. The interior was pitch-dark except for a colored prism that seemed to be magically rotating in the air.

"What the—" Frank muttered.

Phil produced a flashlight from a shoulder bag and flipped it on. He aimed it at the prism, which turned out to be an image on the computer screen.

"It's a screen-saving device," Phil explained, looking at the curved computer screen. "And that's about the coolest convex screen I've ever seen." Phil snapped his fingers and the screen instantly read: WHERE DO YOU WANT TO GO?

"What can I do to help?" Frank asked.

"Nothing," Phil said, sitting in the swivel chair. "Just let me work." Phil then set the flashlight on

74

the desk, aiming the beam at the keyboard. He briefly typed on the keyboard until the screen read: CORNWALL CAVE, ENTER PASSWORD.

"What's Cornwall Cave?" Frank asked.

"It's the place where Merlin, the wizard, was exiled," Phil answered, pulling a floppy disk out of his bag. Next he inserted the disk into the computer's disk drive, hit a few keys, and a stream of words began scrolling across the screen.

"Chances are," Phil explained, "the password is also some sort of medieval reference. So I've made up a special disk to run a lot of them by at a very fast speed. Hopefully, we'll have the magic word pretty soon."

"How soon?" Frank said, worried about Sing's return.

"Five to fifteen minutes," Phil answered. "Relax, all we can do now is wait."

Frank sat on the couch, nervously tapping his foot, while Phil admired the high-tech artistry of Sing's equipment. Finally, after eight minutes, the scrolling data on the screen was replaced by: PASSWORD—BASILISK 3. YOU MAY ENTER THE CAVE.

"Eureka!" Phil cried. "We're in!"

Frank watched the screen as Phil began typing again. Soon the screen read: PROPHECY FAIR: A RE-CREATION OF THE MEDIEVAL PAST FOR THE FUTURE. The lettering started in old-fashioned type and gradually merged into a futuristic font.

"What's Prophecy Fair?" Frank wondered.

"We'll soon find out," Phil said, tapping more keys. Soon the top of the screen read: PROPHECY FAIR PROPOSAL, and Frank and Phil both read through the text on the screen.

The proposal was for a traveling medieval fair that would bear similarities to other medieval and renaissance fairs, such as Avalon, but would also have several futuristic touches. For example, there would be rooms with large screens where participants could interact by computer with a movie set in the medieval world.

"What do you know?" Frank exclaimed. "He *does* want to start his own fair! Okay, can you copy the secret files so we can read them later?"

"That's what this floppy disk is for," Phil said. "We should have the whole thing copied in a minute. Meanwhile, let's take a peek at . . ."

Phil hit more keys and suddenly the screen read: FANTASY JOURNEY. Then the lettering dissolved and the screen showed a lush forest. Trees blew gently in the breeze, and the sound of birds was heard from side speakers.

"Look," Phil said as he tapped a key. "The image is wavering now as if I were cantering on a horse. I bet you can fight and talk to people and all sorts of things. This is amazing!"

"It's getting hot in here," Frank said. "I think I'll feel calmer outside with Callie. Lock the door after me and come out as soon as you're done."

"Will do," Phil said, his eyes glued to the screen.

Frank stepped out of the trailer, relieved to feel the night air. "Find anything?" Callie asked.

76

"Quite a bit," Frank replied. "Our best guess here is looking pretty solid."

"Tell me about it," Callie urged.

"Wait," Frank suddenly whispered. "Someone's coming." Frank knocked behind his back on the trailer door, hoping he was loud enough for Phil to hear, then took Callie's hand. "Come on," Frank said as he began walking with Callie toward a rapidly approaching figure.

As Frank and Callie drew closer to the figure they could see it was Alvin Sing. "Hello there," Sing greeted them as he approached. "Bored with the banquet?"

"No, of course not," Frank said. He remembered how touchy the general manager could be about the fair. He and Callie began walking alongside Sing. "We just wanted a breath of fresh air. It's such a great summer night out here. What did we miss?"

"King Bertram persuaded Sir Damian to join him for supper," Sing answered. "But they will engage in battle tomorrow."

They were nearing the trailer, and Frank could see that was where Sing was headed. Had Phil hidden, Frank wondered, or was he too enthralled with Sing's computer to have heard Frank's knocks?

"You know what bothers me about all this medieval stuff?" Callie said, attempting to stall Sing.

"What's that?" Sing asked, not slackening his pace.

"It seems the women really got the short end of the stick back then," Callie said. "Did any of them have a significant role in their world?"

77

"Some did," Sing answered. "Both Isabella of Spain and Eleanor of Aquitaine were very powerful queens. And then, of course, there was Joan of Arc. But for the most part, women were either hard-working peasants and housewives or beautiful noblewomen to be admired."

They were at the trailer now. "Oh, that's outrageous!" Callie cried, loud enough for Phil to hear. "If you ask me, that's why it took men a thousand years to get out of the Dark Ages!"

"Maybe so," Sing replied with a sly smile. He then pulled out a key and slipped it into the lock on the trailer door. Frank held his breath as Sing turned the key.

9 Castle Attack

Sing opened the door and stepped inside the trailer, with Frank and Callie close behind. The trailer was pitch-black except for the colored prism rotating in the air.

Sing flipped on the lights and carefully looked around. There was no sign of Phil. Wherever Phil is, Frank thought, I hope he stays there.

"Someone's been breaking into my system lately," Sing said. "You can't be too careful." He snapped his fingers to start the computer and began typing on the keyboard. After a moment, he stopped and touched the side of the computer.

Callie glanced at Frank. "What's the matter?" Frank asked Sing.

"I'm checking it for warmth," Sing answered. Frank decided not to press the issue.

Sing switched on his laser printer and began

printing a file. Frank wished he knew what Alvin Sing was thinking. When the file finished printing, Sing collected the pages and escorted Frank and Callie out of the trailer.

"Are you going back to the banquet?" Frank asked casually when they were outside.

"No," Sing replied. "I have an appointment at nine. Good night, you two." Frank watched Sing walk off into the darkness.

"Follow him," Frank said to Callie. "See where he goes and who he meets. Let's hook up at the pizza place around ten."

"I'm going to bill you for my time," Callie joked as she headed after Sing.

Frank immediately started off toward the castle. Then he remembered something—Phil! He made a sharp U-turn and returned to the trailer, picking his way back in.

"Phil," Frank whispered in the darkness. "Coast clear." He heard the trunk open and could just make out Phil climbing out of it.

"There's armor inside there," Phil complained, "and let me tell you it's not very comfortable."

"Hey," Frank retorted, "you're lucky I didn't leave you in there all night."

Phil then left the park to go print out the floppy disk he had copied in a safer place, and Frank ran back to the castle. As Frank entered the Great Hall, he was glad to see the banquet still in progress. No catastrophe yet, he figured as he made his way to Joe's table.

"Just in time for dessert," Joe said. Chet and Iola had joined some other volunteers at another table.

"And I've got some sweet news for you," Frank replied, taking a seat. He quickly filled Joe in on the discovery as they both pretended to watch the Juggler's performance.

"So Sing may be masterminding this and paying Kev Dyson to help him," Joe suggested.

"Maybe," Frank said. "One for profit, one for vengeance. Still a lot of maybes here, though."

As they spoke, Frank and Joe both glanced at Dyson, who was now seated across the hall. A young woman was serving bowls of pudding at the table, and Dyson waved a hand, indicating he didn't want any. The dessert came around the room, and soon Frank and Joe both had a bowl of rice pudding in front of them.

"I'm starving," Frank said, digging into the pudding with a wooden spoon. "How was dinner?"

"The chicken was great," Joe replied. "And guess what? No silverware! We were supposed to eat it with our hands. Aunt Gertrude would have had a fit!" Joe then noticed Frank had an unusual expression on his face.

"What is it?" Joe asked.

"The pudding," Frank gasped. "It's awful. Worse than awful, it's—" But he could find no words to describe the wretched taste in his mouth.

Frank and Joe then noticed other people screwing their faces into strange expressions, and soon a chorus of disgust was heard around the room.

"What's wrong with the pudding?" "Yecch!" "I've never tasted anything so revolting!"

"What's in the pudding?" Joe asked Frank.

"I'm not sure," Frank said. "Taste it."

Joe dipped his spoon into his pudding and sampled a small amount. "Eccch," Joe choked. "It tastes like horseradish!"

People were now spitting out their pudding, and a few were rushing out of the hall. "There's been some mistake," Growtowski called frantically from his table. "Don't eat your pudding! I repeat! Please, don't eat your pudding!"

"Even at discount, this meal's too expensive," a man shouted. "I want my money back!" Other patrons began angrily shouting the same request.

Then suddenly, with a loud flap, a large canvas banner unfurled from the top of the ceiling. Heads glanced up to read the black lettering on the banner, which proclaimed:

Though you may dislike my favorite spice,
You've just begun to feel my weapon slice.
—The Knight of the Flaming Sword

"Come on," Joe said, grabbing Frank's arm. "This could be our chance to get him."

Frank and Joe ran out of the room, dashed up two flights of stone steps, and moved down a corridor on the third level, finally entering a richly furnished bedchamber directly over the Great Hall.

"Look," Frank said, pointing to the holes in the

floor Chet had referred to. "There's rope coming through two of those holes. Someone must have jerked the rope a few moments ago to release the banner."

Frank and Joe quickly left the room and searched up and down the corridor. They saw nothing but the thick stone masonry of the castle walls.

"Hey, wait a second," Joe said, moving to a wall. "There's a rectangular crack in this wall. I saw a prop sword in the bedchamber. Go grab it."

Frank quickly fetched the prop sword, and Joe stuck it into the crack, soon managing to pry open a secret door in the wall. Frank and Joe stooped to enter a dark storage chamber. "Check this," Joe said, finding an empty animal cage on the floor.

"The culprit must have used that for the rabbit," Frank figured. "He probably ditched the cage here rather than risk storing it in a locker."

"I wish we could put *him* in a cage." Joe scowled, frustrated that they had found nothing better.

"Hey, the knight, or whoever he is, is getting bolder with his crusade," Frank observed. "And that just may be the guy's downfall."

"Well, he's long gone now," Joe muttered. "Let's go."

At ten o'clock the Hardys, Chet, and Iola were waiting at their favorite pizza parlor in Bayport when Phil rushed in with a stack of papers.

"Here's the hard copy of Sing's secret file," Phil said, taking a seat. "It's got all sorts of plans for

Prophecy Fair, but nothing actually indicating Sing is behind the sabotage."

"Let me see," Chet said, reaching for the papers with one hand, a slice of pepperoni pizza in the other.

"Careful!" Joe exclaimed. "We don't need grease on our best evidence."

"And didn't you get enough to eat at the banquet?" Iola asked, stirring her pink lemonade.

"If a knight's not hungry, he's not doing his job," Chet announced as he glanced over the pages.

"Oh, by the way," Iola offered, "I still haven't gotten hold of Marcia Segal yet. I've called her a bunch of times, and I even left a message."

"Stay on it," Frank advised.

Just then Callie entered the parlor and hurried over to the table. "Sing met with a man in a hotel lounge," Callie said, pulling up a chair. "The man was dressed in a suit. He looked like a businessman. Sing talked with him awhile then gave him the papers we saw him print. Then I followed Sing back to his motel."

"Maybe Sing met with someone interested in investing in Prophecy Fair," Joe suggested, stealing a pepperoni from Chet.

"Maybe," Frank said thoughtfully. "But everything we have on him is still circumstantial. Joe, I want you to apply some serious pressure to Dyson tomorrow. See if you can get something, anything, out of him. Force it if you have to."

"And while I'm applying pressure to the best

knight since the days of the Round Table, what are you going to be doing?" Joe wanted to know.

"Uncovering the Knight of the Flaming Sword," Frank said.

The sky was an ominous gray the next morning when the Hardys found Growtowski in the mock village, tasting a cup of cider. "I'm just checking everything I can think of," Growtowski explained, a nervous edge to his voice. "Come on, we open soon."

Frank and Joe accompanied Growtowski to his trailer, revealing what they had learned about Sing as they walked. When they entered the trailer, the phone machine was blinking. Growtowski pushed the Play button.

There was a message from a friend, a message from someone interested in buying his medieval sword, and a message from an insurance salesman regarding a certain policy. Growtowski cut the machine off during the last message. Frank and Joe exchanged a look.

"Well, it's time to attire for the day's battle." Growtowski sighed as he opened the trunk where he stored his armor.

An hour later the Avalon knights, all fully armored and armed, were moving through the vast castle. Joe found Chet adjusting his helmet in a corridor. "You missed the briefing yesterday and I'm supposed to fill you in," Chet said, obviously sucking something.

"What's in your mouth?" Joe asked with a grin.

"Lifesaver," Chet explained. "Candy gives me quick energy. Anyway, to win the battle, Sir Damian's men have to capture Iola, or Princess Rowena as she's known around here. She'll be hidden somewhere in the castle, and the rest of us will be stationed all over the place. The more of the enemy we kill, the less chance they'll have of capturing the princess."

"What's my post?" Joe asked, adjusting his elbow armor.

"You're on the eastern front tower," Chet said, slapping Joe's shoulder. "I'll see you later. I need to pick up a few things for the battle."

After trudging up six flights of stone steps, Joe finally stepped outside onto one of the castle's high, rounded towers. Above him, Joe saw dark clouds moving through the sky, and below he saw visitors milling about the field. Attendance was low that day, and Joe figured that was due to a combination of bad weather, bad word of mouth, and Krause's damaging articles.

Joe heard the sound of his breathing inside the helmet. It's lonely inside this armor, he realized.

Suddenly there was a loud rumbling, and Joe saw Sir Damian come thundering out of the forest on horseback, his followers running after him, calling murderously for "Avalon blood!"

When they reached the castle, Sir Damian swung off his horse and the outlaw knights began charging through the great wooden door. Joe heard a splat and saw one of the enemy knights launching cantaloupes at the wall below with a catapult. The castle was under attack!

Moments later a knight wearing black armor rushed onto Joe's tower. Joe's pulse quickened as he realized it was Dyson. With two hands Dyson slashed his sword at Joe, but Joe stopped the blow with his shield.

Joe stepped back, lifting his visor. "So tell me more about Sir Geoffrey," Joe told his foe. "Why are you so stuck on this guy?"

Dyson lifted his visor. "He was one of the great knights of all time," Dyson stated proudly. "A true champion. Like me!" In a flash, Dyson swung his sword low and caught Joe hard on the left leg.

Joe knelt on his "chopped-off" left leg, keeping his eyes on Dyson. "Until he went crazy after the Crusades," Joe challenged. "Then he was mostly just a champion at attacking innocent people."

Dyson's sword froze in midair. "How do you know about that?" Dyson asked gruffly.

"I did my homework," Joe said, suddenly lunging at Dyson. Dyson quickly blocked the shot, then brought his sword around to "chop off" Joe's right arm.

"Great men have great flaws," Dyson said as Joe dropped his shield to the ground.

"Well, you know something," Joe said, switching his sword to his left hand and switching tactics. "Sometimes innocent people *deserve* to be attacked. You know what I mean? And if you do, maybe we should talk. Maybe we should team up instead of trying to kill each other."

Dyson looked at Joe, unsure whether to believe him. Then he started moving toward him. "I'm not going to kill you," Dyson sneered, pulling out a length of rope. "You're not worthy to die by my sword. No, Sir Joe, I'm going to humiliate you by tying you up."

Joe sprang to his feet, but Dyson sent a brutal kick to Joe's breastplate, knocking Joe flat on his back.

"You're supposed to be crippled!" Dyson yelled, and before Joe could make a move, Dyson whipped the rope around Joe's wrists and bound Joe to a bar that ran across a gap in the tower.

"Remember Sir Geoffrey of Martel!" Dyson called as he fled the tower.

Joe tugged furiously at the rope, more convinced than ever Dyson was the mystery knight. He wanted to follow Dyson, but the rope wasn't letting him go. Joe was relieved when Chet appeared on the neighboring tower.

"Hey, Chet!" he yelled. But Chet didn't hear him. Chet was busily performing the knightly ritual of unwrapping a candy bar.

Chet suddenly dropped the candy bar and started backing away from a knight who had appeared on the tower. Like Dyson, the knight wore black armor and carried no shield but, instead of a rattan stick, this knight wielded what seemed to be a genuine sword.

Joe noticed the knight wore no surcoat. Instead an emblem was painted on the knight's breastplate.

Chet began circling away from the knight as the knight slowly lifted the steel sword into the air.

Suddenly lightning streaked the sky, and Joe felt as if the electricity bolted into his heart. In that brief flash, Joe could see the knight's emblem. It was the unmistakable sign of a flaming sword!

10 A Knight to Remember

Gripping his sword with two hands, the Knight of the Flaming Sword took a vicious swipe at Chet's head. Chet blocked the shot with his shield, but the knight came back even harder, knocking the shield right off Chet's arm.

Thunder shook the sky as Joe tugged madly at his rope. Joe felt rain pelting his helmet, and he noticed most of the visitors below were running for the castle or the costume tent across the field.

Again Joe saw the knight swing at Chet, this time cracking Chet's rattan sword in half. Chet dropped his weapon as the knight menacingly poised his sword for another, perhaps deadly, blow.

Chet backed away, but the knight followed. The knight swung but missed. Joe watched Chet backstep all the way to the gap in the tower wall, where

Chet gripped one of the two defense bars running across the gap to keep from toppling over.

The knight swung again, and Chet climbed onto the lower bar to escape the blow. Careful, Chet, Joe urged silently, still struggling with the rope. But as the knight swung again with full force, Chet jerked his helmet back, and to Joe's horror, the momentum pulled Chet backward off the tower!

Joe saw Chet desperately scrape at stone as he fell, finally managing to catch hold of a long metal pole extended from the tower wall. Joe then glimpsed the knight fleeing the tower.

"Help him!" Joe roared, rain pounding his helmet. But no one was around to hear.

Good thing that pole was there, Joe thought. And then it dawned on Joe *why* that pole was there. People in open spaces, like golf courses and parks, were especially vulnerable to electrical storms and so . . . the pole Chet was clinging to was a lightning rod!

"Somebody help!" Joe shouted as loud as he could.

Suddenly Joe saw another knight appear on the neighboring tower and run to the edge. The knight grabbed a bar with his gloved hand and reached out to Chet with his other hand, but he couldn't get near enough. Joe saw the panther emblem on the knight's surcoat and realized it was Kev Dyson.

"Hang on," Dyson yelled, lifting his visor. "I'll get you!"

"Hurry!" Chet screamed back. "I'm losing my grip! It's slippery from the rain!"

91

As the rain poured harder, Joe saw Dyson climb over to the other side of the bar and, still holding it, reach for Chet again. Dyson was closer but not close enough. Again lightning flashed!

Joe gave one final yank at his rope and finally pulled himself free. He flew down the tower steps, dashed across a corridor, and raced up to the neighboring tower. He ran over to Dyson, who was still desperately reaching for Chet.

"Let me try," Joe yelled, tearing off a glove. "I think I've got a longer reach!"

"Okay," Dyson said, giving Joe his place. "I'll hold you!"

Dyson grabbed Joe's left hand and, trusting Dyson's grip, Joe stretched his body over the tower wall as far as he could. His right hand was almost touching Chet's left hand but not quite. Lightning flashed again!

"Chet," Joe yelled to his friend, "you've got to give me your left hand! Come on, you can do it!"

Chet took a deep breath, let go with his left hand, and reached it through the slashing rain toward Joe, who instantly gripped it. Dyson then grabbed Joe around the waist, and together they pulled Chet's hefty bulk to the safety of the tower.

Greatly relieved, the three knights pulled off their helmets, letting the rain rush over their faces. "The original Sir Geoffrey lost his grip," Joe told Dyson, "but maybe you haven't lost yours."

"I'm not really insane," Dyson said, almost smiling. "I just get into my part pretty intensely. By the way, sorry about that kick."

"Here, have a Lifesaver," Chet said, gratefully extending the pack to Dyson. "As many as you want!"

"And why don't you tell me," Joe said, "who you were meeting at the filling station two days ago."

Caught off guard, Dyson stared at Joe. Then he sighed, and the three knights made their way down the tower stairs.

Unaware what had been happening above, Frank was roving through the castle, searching everywhere for a clue that might break the case. Along with a few other visitors, Frank stopped in a corridor to watch the fearsome Sir Damian single-handedly battle two Avalon knights.

Hearing another knight clambering down a flight of steps, Frank turned and his heart skipped a beat when he saw a flaming sword emblem on the knight's breastplate. He also noticed that the knight carried what looked like a real sword.

After seeing the direction in which the Knight of the Flaming Sword was running, Frank guessed he'd be heading for the secret room.

Now's my chance! Frank thought. He quickly raced down one flight of stairs and ran up the stairs on the opposite side. Made it! Frank thought. He crouched on a high stone ledge across the corridor from the secret room, watching. Before long, the knight appeared, and by slipping his sword through the crack, pried the door open, then disappeared inside the chamber.

Frank lowered himself down from the ledge and

peered through the door's crack. All Frank could make out was a shadow moving in darkness. The shadow seemed to be removing his helmet, but in spite of squinting, Frank could see no features of the face. Frustrated, he realized all he could do was wait.

Frank moved back to the steps, walked up a few, and waited. Soon he saw the stone door open and someone stepped out of it. The someone was wearing a skirt—a serving girl's costume—and Frank realized it was Carla!

Carrying a duffel bag, Carla began descending the steps on the other side of the corridor. Frank began descending on his side. At this point, he figured it was wiser to see where she led him rather than confront her.

On the first level, Frank saw Carla walk out of a side door, and he trailed her, carefully keeping his distance. Outside the rain had stopped, leaving the air fresh and cool, and people were beginning to mill about again.

Carla stopped at a pay phone near the castle and Frank slid behind a tree to observe her. She picked up the receiver, dropped a quarter in the slot, and began pressing numbers. Straining to see, Frank managed to catch the last two digits of the phone number by their location on the grid. The digits were 2 and 4.

Carla listened a moment, looking around furtively. Frank edged behind the tree, not wanting to be caught now. This conversation could be crucial, he thought.

"Hi," Carla said into the receiver, "it's me."

There was a pause while the other party spoke.

"Yes, I . . . I just did it," Carla said, her voice sounding troubled. She paused and then took a deep breath.

"I'll tell you what's the matter," Carla said, her voice wavering. "I'm scared. This was worse than the others. Someone was almost—" Frank guessed she'd been interrupted on the other end.

"No, you don't understand," he heard her say, "I want out of this! I went along at first, but now I want out!"

There was a longer pause. "No, I don't want you to do that. Please. You know I don't." Carla's pleading stopped for a moment as the other person spoke.

"All right, I'll stay with it if I have to," she said. "I'll help you get what you want." She paused once more.

"Yes, I will be strong. Just like Joan of Arc. And I will never tell anyone who you are." Her voice sounded stronger now. "I promise. Goodbye."

Carla hung up the receiver, a determined look on her face. Now she looked more like the girl he'd seen jumping the chestnut horse, Frank thought. There's more than one side to this girl, he realized, and the person on the other end of that phone line is somehow manipulating her. But who is it?

Carla began walking and Frank followed, even more determined not to nab her since she seemed so eager to keep her partner's identity a secret.

Carla passed two knights slashing at each other in

the wet grass near the castle, then began cutting across the field. She soon came to the mock village.

Carla passed by the Juggler, who was now keeping three large knives in the air, and continued on past the wild-haired Enchantress. Perhaps Carla's going to the Drench a Wench booth, Frank speculated.

The Enchantress turned her palm upward—and a ball of flame exploded in her hand. But this was no special effect. The Enchantress screamed, and Frank realized the flame was bigger than before and was licking at her gauzy sleeve. The fire was dancing its way up her arm!

11 Enter the King

Frank tackled the Enchantress to the ground and threw himself on her burning sleeve. He felt a burst of heat on his shirt, then felt it subside.

"Are you okay?" Frank asked as Joe stood up. He glanced around for Carla, but she was nowhere in sight.

"I think it's just a minor burn." The Enchantress winced and pulled a pouch from a fold in her gown. "Could you get some ointment out of here?"

Frank unzipped the pouch, figuring there would be plenty of opportunity to catch up with Carla. He reached in and found the tube of ointment in the bottom of the pouch, but when he pulled it out, a piece of parchment was stuck to it. He removed the parchment, but couldn't help seeing what was written on it.

By now I think you know my fearsome name,
And now this little fair shall die in flame!
    —The Knight of the Flaming Sword

Frank stuck the note in his back pocket, then began rubbing ointment on the Enchantress's burned arm.

"Someone must have slipped a different type of flash paper into my pouch," the Enchantress said. "It looked okay, but . . ."

"Maybe someone broke into your locker last night," Frank suggested.

"Who's doing this?" the Enchantress demanded, her heavily made-up eyes flashing with anger.

"I wish I knew," Frank answered. After all, he only had half the story.

Meanwhile, above Chet's protests, Dyson insisted on a quick trip to the infirmary. "I'll catch up with you guys later," Joe said. "There's something I need to do."

Joe hurried to the locker room, figuring the Knight of the Flaming Sword might be in there changing or storing his armor. Instead, he saw someone in a monk's robe attempting to pry open a locker with a prop sword. Joe figured this was probably the same guy he had chased twice before. Then he realized that the guy was breaking into *his* locker!

"Can I help you, sir?" Joe called, throwing the door open.

The monk wheeled around to face Joe, the hood

shadowing his face, then dashed out of the room through another door.

"Oh, no you don't!" Joe yelled, chasing after the monk. "Not this time, pal!"

Joe chased the monk up five flights of castle steps, then across a corridor. Rushing past two knights whacking at each other, Joe ducked, and a sword went rolling by his feet. "Thanks," Joe said, scooping up the weapon as he ran.

Just as Joe saw the monk disappear up the last flight of steps, Sir Damian came barreling down the corridor, dragging Princess Rowena by the wrist. "Don't let him capture me," Princess Rowena screamed, "I'm the king's daughter!"

Joe stopped, hearing the pleading of his girlfriend, Iola. But she was just playing a role, Joe realized, and the monk was dangerously real. Joe dashed up the last flight of steps until he felt fresh air and found himself again atop one of the towers.

The monk was waiting for him. He slashed at Joe with the prop sword, but Joe launched a powerful backhand with his newfound weapon and sent the monk's sword sailing over the tower wall. Joe strode toward the defenseless monk, who backed toward the edge of the tower.

"You don't want to go that way," Joe warned. "Trust me."

The monk glanced over the tower's edge and stopped moving.

"And now for the unveiling," Joe said, thrusting back the monk's hood with his sword. Staring back at Joe was Krause, furiously chewing his gum.

99

"Krause!" Joe exclaimed. "What are you after?"

"The same thing you're after," Krause said, panting. "A good story!"

"Have you just been *looking* for a story," Joe challenged, brandishing his weapon, "or have you been making one?"

"Meaning what?" Krause countered.

"Meaning you've just become my number-one suspect as the instigator of a series of very dangerous crimes. Now, would you like to explain yourself here or would you rather wait for the inquisition at the police station?"

"Wait," Krause protested. "I'm no criminal. I was just looking for the messages."

"What messages?" Joe pressed.

"The messages you and your brother keep finding," Krause answered. "That's what I was looking for in your locker."

"And I suppose you were looking for the messages in my house, too?" Joe inquired, keeping his weapon ready.

"That's right, I was," Krause said. "If I can read those notes, you see, I might be able to figure out who's sabotaging the fair. A good reporter is also part detective, you know."

"Is that a fact?" Joe scoffed. "Now tell me why you paid Kev Dyson to give you inside information on the fair."

Krause popped his gum. "He's been to the fair the last few years, and I thought he might be able to shed some light on things," Krause explained. "I met him at the filling station because I didn't want you guys horning in on us. You horned in, anyway."

"And why did you leave the bloody glove and threatening message in my room?" Joe demanded.

"To scare you and your brother away once and for all," Krause stated. "Look, it was driving me nuts being scooped by two punks from a school newspaper. I'm new at the *Star,* and if I don't make a name for myself fast I'll be stuck covering supermarket openings and traffic court forever!"

"How did you know to put the message in verse?" Joe persisted.

"I caught a glimpse of one those notes before your brother hid it from me," Krause explained. "I could see it was a couplet. I just couldn't read all of it."

Joe remembered that the message in the bedroom was missing the knight's name. "Okay," Joe said, finally lowering his sword. "I believe you. And I won't turn you over to the cops if you agree not to put another damaging article about the fair in tomorrow's paper."

"Sorry," Krause said, adjusting his robe. "I don't cave in to blackmail. Besides, Hardy, the public has a right to know what's happening around here. Maybe people shouldn't be coming to the fair if it's so dangerous. Ever think of that? Journalists aren't complete jerks, you know."

"Well, maybe you're right," Joe admitted reluctantly. "Oh, one more thing. Who's Marcia Segal?"

"She's a friend of mine," Krause told him. "My

car was in the shop that day so I borrowed hers. That was pretty savvy of you to trace her name. Maybe there's a little detective in you after all."

"Thanks," Joe replied. If you only knew, he thought.

Hearing a familiar voice, Joe glanced over the wall to view Sir Damian galloping away on horseback with his girlfriend. "I have captured the princess!" Sir Damian called to the dark sky. "Sir Damian has conquered!"

"How about we climb down from here before I get a nosebleed?" Krause suggested.

"Sure," Joe said. Together they made their way down the tower steps. On reaching the bottom, Krause apologized for the bloody glove stunt and wandered off.

Joe hoped his brother had had better luck tracking the mystery knight. He soon came to the field where a crowd of visitors and weary, battle-worn knights were gathered around King Bertram and Sir Damian. "Sir Damian has captured my daughter and therefore has won the battle," King Bertram announced. "However, I have made him an offer and he has accepted.

"Tomorrow my knights will challenge his knights in a tournament of champions," the king continued. "If his side triumphs, I surrender my reign of all England to him. If my knights win, Sir Damian must become my loyal follower. Tomorrow all will be decided!"

Joe found Frank in the crowd, and the brothers

hurried away to share their recent discoveries. "So the only question left," Frank said, "is, who was Carla talking to?"

"I have an idea, and I hope I'm wrong," Joe said, "but remember the message that we heard in Growtowski's trailer?"

"From the insurance salesman," Frank replied.

"Why did he cut it off in the middle?" Joe asked.

"Either because he wasn't interested," Frank guessed, "or because he didn't want us to hear it."

"Let's go," Joe said.

Frank and Joe ran to the trailer, and when no one answered Frank's knock, he picked his way in. Inside the trailer, Frank and Joe immediately went to the phone.

"Look," Frank said, pointing to a number printed below the dial buttons. "The number here is 555-2624."

"It ends in 24," Joe noted. "Just like the number Carla called."

Frank played around with the phone machine and finally found the insurance message. Apparently Growtowski had called the insurance company about a policy that would reimburse him in the event his fair suffered a bad season, and the salesman was getting back to Growtowski with more specifics on the policy.

"Well, what do you think?" Joe said after a long moment.

"Maybe Mr. Growtowski is sabotaging his own fair to collect the insurance payoff," Frank said thoughtfully. "Since he's in financial trouble, maybe he figures that's the best way to pull in a lot of cash fast."

"He sure was reluctant to call in the police a few days ago," Joe added.

"And maybe he put us on Sing's trail," Frank speculated, "to keep us off the real scent."

"I've seen Growtowski with Carla," Joe added. "She seems to follow him pretty obediently."

"Of course, that could be just because he's her boss," Frank pointed out.

"Could be," Joe agreed. "Or it could be that he's the voice on the other end of that telephone line."

The Hardys next looked for Carla, but apparently she had left the park, and though the brothers spoke to several fair employees, no one could shed much light on Carla's personal life. At closing time Frank and Joe observed the eagle swooping down to the falconer's glove one last time, and they left the fair and decided to get some dinner.

From a booth in a diner, the Hardys watched the dusk deepen and the highway lights turn on. Through the window Joe noticed a fine mist in the air.

"All right, let's review what we have," Frank said, setting down his turkey club sandwich. "We know Carla is causing the acts of terror, and we know someone is manipulating her into doing it. But who? And why?"

"I'm pretty sure Krause was telling me the truth," Joe stated. "And there's no way Carla could have been calling Kev Dyson. He was with me at the time. It could be Growtowski or it still could be

Sing. He answers the telephone in the trailer too, remember."

"Or it could be someone we haven't even thought of yet," Frank suggested.

"Or even met," Joe said, dipping a french fry in ketchup. "So we're still stuck in the mud, aren't we?"

"Carla's the key," Frank concluded. "After dinner let's pay a visit to her motel room. If she's there, let's question her. If she's not, let's find whatever clues we can."

A half hour later Frank and Joe drove to the Sleepy Knight motel, where the Avalon staff was staying for the week. The Hardys drove past the colored banners that flew over the parking lot and parked their van in a vacant lot adjacent to the motel.

The mist tickled their skin as Frank and Joe climbed a flight of steps up to the motel's balcony. After knocking on Carla's door and getting no answer, Frank set to work picking the lock.

"Frank, stop," Joe whispered, and Frank turned to see someone approaching from the other end of the balcony. Both Hardys noticed the person was clutching a wicked-looking medieval weapon in one hand—a flail with a spiked ball.

"He's holding that weapon like he knows how to use it," Joe observed quietly.

"Don't think I haven't noticed," Frank replied.

As the figure came nearer, slightly swinging the spiked ball, the Hardys realized it was none other than the king himself—Art Growtowski!

12 Pathway to Evil

"Hello, boys," Growtowski said as he approached. "I didn't realize it was you here."

"We thought you were spending the nights in your trailer," Joe commented.

"I have been," Growtowski replied. "But I don't sleep very well there, and I desperately need some rest. So I hired a security guard to watch the grounds tonight."

Growtowski looked haggard. To Joe the man seemed to have aged a few years over the past week. "Were you sleeping with that thing?" Joe asked, indicating the spiked weapon.

"Oh, this," Growtowski said, lifting the flail. "I've taken to keeping a weapon nearby. Who knows? If someone is trying to destroy my fair they might also want to destroy me."

The Hardys watched Growtowski, trying to read

him. "How's the financial situation after today?" Frank asked.

"Pretty bad," Growtowski confessed. "I've lost a lot from the heavy advertising and the discounts and the jousters and the refunds. And then today was an especially poor turnout. I'm deep in the red now and unless tomorrow is a very big day I'll be forced to do something drastic."

"Like what?" Joe asked casually. "Close the fair and collect an insurance payoff?"

"Collect insurance?" Growtowski asked, taken aback. "Why, no. I was considering taking out a recovery policy, but it was quite expensive and didn't offer much indemnity for my type of situation."

Frank and Joe both wondered if this explanation got Growtowski off the hook. "Then what did you mean by drastic?" Frank questioned.

"I have one option left," Growtowski said with a deep sigh. "Sell my grandfather's sword. I've resisted offers for years, some of them pretty high, but if I sell the sword I'll have enough to keep Avalon running just fine. It'll hurt me terribly to do it, but it would kill me to lose the fair."

"The sword . . ." Frank repeated to himself. Joe glanced at his brother.

Just then the Juggler came up the steps, waved, and let himself into his room.

"Mr. Growtowski," Frank suddenly asked, "does the sword have a name?"

"Yes, it does," Growtowski answered. "It's called the Chauvency. That's because it was found inside

Chauvency castle in France. It dates back to the thirteenth century. Why do you ask?"

"I'm not sure yet," Frank responded.

"So what are you boys doing here?" Growtowski asked, swinging the spiked ball a bit.

"We thought we might find a missing piece of the puzzle from Sing," Joe answered quickly. No sense in letting him know they were investigating Carla if she and Growtowski were working together, he figured.

"Well, you're one door off," Growtowski said. "He's in Room 229." Growtowski turned and trudged wearily to his room.

"Why did you ask the sword's name?" Joe asked as soon as Growtowski was out of earshot.

"I'll tell you in a sec," Frank said, continuing to pick the lock on Carla's door. Soon Frank and Joe entered the room and flipped on the lights. Frank immediately found an address book on the nightstand, and Joe began examining a stack of books on the dresser.

"These books are all about knights and related subjects like horsemanship and weaponry," Joe noted. "Carla made a comment one day about how Mr. Growtowski wouldn't allow girls to be knights. She didn't make much of it, but I think she really wants to be a knight. And, boy, when she puts that armor on she really turns into one. A pretty awesome one. Maybe that's why she's been doing this."

"Maybe her anger is part of it," Frank said as he jotted something in his memo pad. "But I think there's more. On the phone, Carla said, 'I'll help you get what you want.'"

"What did you find there?" Joe asked.

"Uncle Tommy," Frank answered. "Whose phone number happens to end in '24.' Let's go."

The Hardys quickly left the room, went down the stairs from the balcony, and began walking toward the vacant lot. "Here's what I'm thinking," Frank said, keeping his voice low. "Maybe we've been looking at this case all wrong. We've been looking for someone with a motive to destroy Avalon. I mean, everything points to that—the accidents, the messages. But maybe that's not what the bad guy is after."

"Then what *is* he after?" Joe asked impatiently.

"Maybe he wants to bleed Mr. Growtowski financially," Frank explained, "so Mr. Growtowski will be forced to sell the Chauvency, his treasured medieval sword. A lot of people have tried to buy it, but up until now he's never considered selling it. Now, finally, he may have to."

"So all the sabotage isn't so much to drive people *away* as to make Growtowski spend a lot of money to *keep* them coming," Joe said.

"Maybe so," Frank replied.

"But who would want the sword so badly they'd go to all this trouble?" Joe wanted to know.

Before Frank could answer, the Hardys saw two greenish bolts of electricity appear near where their van was parked. The mix of mist and darkness made it difficult for them to see much else.

"What was that?" Frank whispered.

As Frank and Joe moved closer, they saw two hands thrust forward and two more bolts of electricity seem to zip out.

"Hey, watch it," Joe called. "That's our van!" Frank and Joe had now come close enough to make out Alvin Sing's face in the mist.

"I'm trying to make it disappear," Sing quipped. "Then perhaps I'll make you disappear."

"Real funny," Joe said, unamused.

"Almost as funny as breaking into someone's secret files," Sing returned. "Which I know you did the other night because of the little gnomes inside my computer. I also know you've been tapping into the Avalon system for the past month."

"Wait," Frank said, suddenly more interested. "I admit we've broken into your system twice this past week, but that's it. Are you positive someone's been tapping in for a month?"

"I'm quite positive," Sing replied. "First at our home office in Connecticut and now here. And if it isn't you, I'd like to know who it is."

"So would I," Frank said, heading for the van. "Come on, Joe, let's hit the road."

"But I want to know what he's doing zapping those bolts of electricity," Joe protested. "And what other devious wizardry he's up to."

"The bolts are a trick I'm experimenting with," Sing said, unrolling a thin plastic strip from his wrist. "A small laser machine is over there on the ground."

110

"Tricks to use at Prophecy Fair," Joe accused. "To make it better than Avalon."

"Perhaps," Sing replied with a thin smile.

"He's a wizard all right," Frank called, "but he's not the evil one. Come on, brother, let's go."

Joe climbed into the driver side of the van and began steering out of the lot while Frank pulled a stack of papers from the glove compartment. "Where to?" Joe asked.

"Phil's house," Frank replied, scanning through the papers.

"Mind telling me what's going on?" Joe asked.

"This is the printout from the entire Avalon system," Frank answered. "I've gone over it a few times since Phil first brought it over. I noticed a file called 'Chauvency,' which contained a bunch of names and dates and numbers. I didn't realize it then, but I see now these are people who have made offers to buy the Chauvency sword over the years."

"And you think one of them might be the person controlling Carla?" Joe asked.

"Yes, I do," Frank said, suddenly pointing to a name on a sheet. "Especially since one of them is named Tommy Morslip. And Mr. Morslip has the same phone number as the person listed in Carla's book as 'Uncle Tommy'!"

"The one whose number ends in '24,'" Joe said, his interest growing.

"And guess what?" Frank said, still reading. "This guy has tried to buy the sword at least fifteen times over the past four years. And look, it says here he's an antique weapons dealer."

"Maybe he's been tapping into the Avalon computer system," Joe concluded, "so he could check the fair's finances and know exactly how much he had to make Mr. Growtowski bleed."

"You got it!" Frank said, slapping the dashboard in triumph.

The Hardys soon arrived at Phil's house, and in no time Phil was on the computer tapping into Tommy Morslip's computer system to check a few things. Phil then armed the Hardys with some equipment and extensive advice, and Frank and Joe drove home, feeling they might be close to ending this mystery.

"Cloudy again," Joe observed as he leaned out the van window. It was early Sunday morning, and the Hardys were back on a highway, headed for Tommy Morslip's home in a rural area about twenty-five miles from Bayport.

Over the radio they heard, ". . . and today is your last chance to catch the Avalon medieval fair in Windsor Park. Today you can see the Tournament of Champions, which will commence at twelve noon . . ."

"And today's our last chance to catch the Knight of the Flaming Sword," Joe added.

"This is it," Frank said as he turned off the highway and began driving down a winding road that led through woods and farmland and finally to an odd-looking house standing on a hill.

The Hardys parked their van a short distance away and walked back toward the house. Frank gave a low whistle as he gazed at the two-story clapboard house with Gothic arches and gables. Ivy grew wildly around the house like a giant serpent trying to enter the windows.

"The Addams Family wouldn't go in here," Joe joked.

"No," Frank said after a deep breath, "but the Hardy brothers are about to."

Frank and Joe walked up a pathway to the front door, and Joe banged a bronze knocker in the shape of a gargoyle. After a long wait, the door opened and a short man wearing a tweed blazer and turtleneck stood in the doorway. Early thirties, Joe guessed. Frank thought there was something both sinister and familiar about the man.

"Are you Tommy Morslip?" Frank inquired.

"Yes, I am," Morslip replied, looking with curiosity at the Hardys.

"Sorry to bother you," Frank said. "But my brother and I are doing an article for the school paper about the medieval fair, and we understand you might have some medieval weapons we can look at. If it's not too much trouble, of course."

"Well, this is rather unexpected," Morslip said. He hesitated a moment. Then he seemed to make a decision. "I suppose I could show you what I have. Follow me."

Morslip began walking down the front hallway of his home. Frank and Joe exchanged a surprised look. The weapons dealer had a slight limp, one they'd seen before. Uncle Tommy was the beggar they had seen at the fair!

113

13 A Dangerous Tour

The limp clinched it for Joe. The beggar had been present at a number of incidents. So the guy had means and motive. And what he couldn't do, Carla could take care of, and he'd be on hand making sure she was doing his dirty work. Joe tried to catch Frank's eye, but his brother shot him a warning look. Joe knew they needed concrete evidence before they could confront Morslip. Well, maybe now they'd get it.

Moving through the house, Frank and Joe noticed most of the furnishings were antiques. One room, however, was a modern office. Frank noticed a computer sitting on a desk by the window.

"How did you find me?" Morslip asked as he led the Hardys up a staircase.

"We were given your name by Art Growtowski,"

114

Joe answered. "The owner of the Chauvency sword."

"I see," Morslip replied. "Well, I'm always glad to give my tour of historical destruction."

On the second floor, Morslip led the Hardys to a door with three high-security locks. "Can't be too careful," Morslip quipped as he fiddled with various keys.

"Wow," Frank said, gaping when the door was finally opened.

The weapons room was covered floor to ceiling with daggers, swords, rapiers, machetes, spears, pikes, pistols, rifles, blunderbusses, cannons, machine guns, and still more weapons. A long shelf contained all sorts of military helmets, and one wall was adorned with at least fifty types of arrows.

There were also pictures, ranging from sketches of Roman warriors to black-and-white photographs of World War II tanks. There was even a color poster of an atomic bomb explosion.

"This is incredible," Joe murmured, overwhelmed.

"Thank you," Morslip replied with a modest nod.

"I didn't realize antique weapons were such a big business," Frank said, admiring an intricately carved samurai bow.

"You'd be surprised," Morslip answered. "Man has always been fascinated by violence."

"Well, I guess collecting weapons is better than actually using them," Frank said, shifting his gaze to a trunk labeled Trick Weapons.

"Of course," Morslip agreed. "And most of my buyers are the most harmless of individuals. For example, an accountant came here the other day. A man who does nothing but tabulate numbers at a desk. And he purchased a dozen of these."

Morslip held up an iron object resembling a pine cone. "It's a German model hand grenade from World War One," Morslip explained. He then pulled out the pin intended to activate the grenade. "Here, catch!" he said, tossing Joe the grenade.

Surprised, Joe caught the deadly object. After a stunned moment, he tossed it back to Morslip. "Do any of these weapons actually work?" he asked.

"What do you say we find out?" Morslip grinned, picking up a long-barreled pistol. "Gentlemen, this is the original Colt revolver, circa 1860, the most popular gun in the Old West."

Morslip fanned back the hammer and aimed the pistol at a target across the room. He then pulled the trigger, and a deafening shot rattled the windows.

"Sorry," Morslip said, "gunshots are so noisy indoors."

"What's this?" Joe said, pointing to a black cannon on the floor, the iron mostly corroded with rust.

"That's from the port of an eighteenth-century Spanish warship," Morslip said, kneeling down. He then launched into a brief history of the cannon, but neither Frank nor Joe failed to notice that he continued to hold onto the pistol. Does he know why we're really here? Frank and Joe each wondered. "May I use your rest room?" Frank asked when the lecture ended.

"Certainly," Morslip replied. "It's just down the hall."

"Thanks," Frank said as he left the room. Hearing Morslip begin to describe the fine points of an African spear, Frank quietly moved down the stairs and went to Morslip's office.

Frank flipped on the computer and began following instructions Phil had written out on a piece of paper. Morslip can't know who we are, Frank reasoned as he worked, or he wouldn't let me roam the house so freely. And he's so into his collection, Joe can easily keep him talking for another ten minutes or so.

Frank lifted his shirt and pulled out a floppy disk and slipped it into the side of the computer, then typed a few keys. If there was any evidence Morslip had been tapping into Avalon's system, it would soon be copied onto the disk. And the Hardys would have their man.

Frank sat back, waiting for the copy process to finish. Upstairs he could hear Morslip rambling on about his precious weapons.

After a few minutes the copy process was completed, and Frank returned to the weapons room. "I snooped around a little bit," Frank confessed to Morslip. "It's an interesting house."

"Thank you," Morslip said, setting down a well-worn Thompson submachine gun. "It belonged to my mother, and most of the furnishings are heirlooms from her family."

"Your collection is amazing," Joe said. "But so far we haven't seen anything from the Middle Ages."

"I have some replicas of medieval objects," Morslip said, tossing Joe a bronze-colored helmet, "but, alas, I don't have anything that is actually of that period."

"Why not?" Joe asked, running a hand over the helmet.

"Because very few weapons of that period exist," Morslip explained. "We're talking about weapons that suffered tremendous abuse in battle hundreds and hundreds of years ago. If they weren't broken to bits then, time has long since buried them or rusted them down to nothing."

"And I suppose the few that have survived are owned mostly by museums," Joe guessed.

"That's right," Morslip answered. "With a few exceptions, such as Mr. Growtowski's sword."

"I guess a weapon that was truly from the Middle Ages would go for big bucks on the open market," Frank speculated.

"You have no idea," Morslip said with a sudden gleam in his eye. "There are collectors out there who would pay a veritable fortune to own a sword that actually touched the hand of a knight."

"I'll bet you'd like to broker a deal on one of those," Joe said with a chuckle.

"You bet your life I would," Morslip said, shifting the Colt pistol to his other hand. "However, if you boys are really interested in the medieval period you must see my display in the basement."

"We'd love to," Frank said, glancing at his watch,

"but the fair's opening soon, and we need to get there. Joe's one of the knights, and he's not supposed to be late."

"It will only take a minute," Morslip persisted, gesturing toward the door with his pistol. "After all, isn't that what you came here to see?"

"It's not that we're uninterested—" Joe started.

"Please," Morslip cut in, gesturing more emphatically with the pistol. "I really must insist."

Frank and Joe looked at each other, both with the same thought. If he doesn't know about us, why raise his suspicions? If he does know about us, he'll shoot us if we don't play along.

"I guess we can spare a minute," Joe said.

Morslip led the Hardys back down the steps, then opened a door and led the boys down a stairwell into the basement. "More security," Morslip mentioned as he unlocked a padlock on a large wooden door. He then slid back a thick wooden bolt and ushered the Hardys into a completely dark room.

Morslip pushed a button, and suddenly monks were heard chanting in low, ominous tones. Morslip pushed another button and the room was illuminated by burning torches angled into the walls. All sorts of ancient and dangerous devices were now visible by the flickering torchlight.

"This is a perfect replica of a Spanish Inquisition torture chamber," Morslip intoned. "Technically the Inquisition was a few years after the Middle Ages, but I think it's close enough to be of interest."

"A bit too close," Joe whispered. Frank nodded.

"I'm very proud of this room," Morslip continued, shadows wavering across his face. "Allow me to show you a few of my favorite devices."

Morslip walked to a sinister contraption consisting of wood, metal, chains, and a wheel. "You may have heard of the rack, but I doubt you've ever seen one," Morslip said gleefully. "When this wheel is turned the body is stretched by the chains until most of the muscles and tendons are ripped apart."

"Ouch," Frank said.

"A wicked device," Morslip said with a grin.

"I hate to break up a party," Joe said, "but we'd better be heading out."

"Oh, just one more thing," Morslip urged, still gripping the pistol.

"Well, if you insist," Frank said without much enthusiasm.

"I do," Morslip returned.

Frank still couldn't tell if Morslip was onto them or not. He certainly seemed as if he was up to no good, but Tommy Morslip was probably always up to no good. After all, this was a man who had a torture chamber in his basement—and was proud of it!

The Hardys followed Morslip to a large rectangular table. "It's called the pendulum," Morslip said, gesturing up at a crescent-shaped blade of steel that hung from the ceiling. The curved bottom edge of the pendulum looked as if it might be sharp.

"How does it work?" Joe asked, not really wanting to know. He figured the sooner Morslip gave his talk, the sooner they could get out of there.

"I'm so glad you asked," Morslip responded. "But it's difficult to describe. It's so much easier to demonstrate. Why don't you both lie down on the table? One of you put your head at one end, the other put your head at the other end."

"We really don't have time for this," Frank protested.

"Lie down," Morslip said, his face now dead serious. His finger fondled the pistol's trigger.

Reluctantly Joe climbed onto the table and lay down. Then Frank climbed onto the table and lay down facing in the opposite direction. Leather bindings resembling belts were attached to the table and Morslip proceeded to buckle Frank and Joe's ankles and wrists to the table with one hand, continuing to hold the gun with the other.

"Now, *voilà!*" Morslip said, pushing a button. The pendulum above began to move. Back and forth it swung from a rod, automated by a small motor.

"It works just like the one in the Edgar Allan Poe story," Morslip elaborated. "As the pendulum swings back and forth, it slowly lowers. When the pendulum comes down far enough, it begins to sever the victim, or victims, in half."

"You could have four Hardys for the price of two," Joe joked.

"Psychologically it's very disturbing," Morslip continued. "Most victims of the Inquisition would break down and confess to heresy before the pendulum was halfway down."

Frank and Joe noticed the pendulum was indeed lowering as it silently swung back and forth.

"This has been very educational," Frank said, "but we should be going now."

"That's right," Joe agreed. "I really can't afford to be late today."

"I understand," Morslip responded. "But I'm afraid you'll have to excuse me a moment. I think I hear my telephone ringing upstairs."

"Maybe you could just unstrap us first," Frank suggested.

"No, I'd better get the telephone first," Morslip insisted, moving to the door. "It's the telephone in my office. The one on my desk. Certainly you noticed it when you were in there, Frank."

Frank felt the bottom drop out of his stomach. Morslip knows, he realized.

"How did you know he was in there?" Joe called, trying to keep Morslip in the room.

"I have this little device," Morslip said, pulling out a small object resembling a pager. "It's part of my security system. They're doing wonderful things with security these days, you know. It beeps whenever someone enters a room in the house, and it can even tell me which room they're entering."

"So I was in your office," Frank admitted. "I told you I was snooping around."

"We're amateur reporters," Joe reminded Morslip. "Reporters are notoriously curious."

"Yes, they are," Morslip agreed. "But unfortunately you aren't amateur reporters. You're something even worse—amateur detectives. And I'm sorry to say, you're a little too good at it for your own good."

"What makes you think we're detectives?" Joe asked.

"I saw you sniffing around the fair, examining the accidents," Morslip explained. "So I did a little detective work of my own, and I soon discovered Frank and Joe Hardy were quite the team of teenage supersleuths. 'Were' being the operative word here." Again Morslip walked to the door.

"You're not a very nice man, are you?" Frank called. He wanted to keep Morslip from leaving.

"I'm a determined man," Morslip corrected. "For years I've tried to purchase the Chauvency. I have a buyer ready to give me close to a million dollars for it. But since Mr. Growtowski refuses to sell it and since museums also have good security systems, I was forced to find another way."

"So you found a way to put the financial slash on Growtowski," Joe said, "forcing him to sell the sword."

"And it's all worked out rather well," Morslip boasted. "I had intended to tip off the local paper, but Charlie Krause was already there and he fit into my plan beautifully."

Above the Hardys the pendulum was still swinging, still lowering.

"And you don't care how many people get hurt by your plan?" Frank taunted. "Not even if one of them is your niece, Carla?"

"Carla's not being hurt by this," Morslip angrily shot back.

"You're forcing her to be the Knight of the Flaming Sword," Joe retorted. "And she's really upset about it!"

"Carla was a painfully shy child with no friends," Morslip said emphatically. "So I got the girl interested in medieval history. She was fascinated by the knights. Growtowski won't allow her to be a knight, but I will! So don't tell me about forcing!"

"What are you making her do today?" Frank asked.

"I'd rather not say," Morslip said, turning to Frank. "But I can tell you, it's big. People will ask for refunds, and I wouldn't be surprised if there are a few lawsuits. Especially when people discover the brave Hardy boys decided to handle this case themselves rather than bringing in the police."

"If the police had come, you would have backed off and tried again in another town," Joe said, straining to break his binding. "You would never have left Avalon in peace."

"No, not until I get the Chauvency," Morslip returned, his voice taking on a determined edge. Then once again he moved to the door.

"People know we're here," Frank shouted. "You'll never get away with this!"

"I'll get away with it," Morslip assured them, his hand on the doorknob. "And now, Frank and Joe, I appreciate your trying to keep me here and talk me out of the day's destruction, but I really must go. Just yell if you need anything."

Morslip left the room, and the Hardys heard the wooden bolt being slid across the door. Frank and

Joe both jerked at the leather binding for several desperate minutes, but it wasn't giving an inch.

The chanting of the monks seemed to grow louder, the torches seemed to burn brighter.

"The pendulum's about halfway down," Joe said, gazing up at the swinging blade. Back and forth, back and forth the crescent swung, the steady motion almost hypnotizing Joe. He realized the pendulum would stop for nothing. "What now?" Joe demanded.

"I have no idea," Frank answered quietly.

14 Close Shave

"Maybe it's not really sharp," Joe said, staring up at the blade. "After all, it's just a replica."

"Whether it is or not," Frank replied, "Morslip's right about one thing."

"What's that?" Joe inquired.

"It *is* psychologically disturbing."

As the pendulum continued swinging, the monks chanted and the torches flickered and danced. Frank felt sweat trickling down his temple while Joe felt it more under his arms.

Joe tugged furiously at his binding again but again nothing gave. On the other side of the table, Frank lay still, contemplating the pendulum above.

"I forget," Joe said, exhausted from his effort. "How did the guy escape in the Poe story?"

"He managed to rub some meat on his binding,"

126

Frank said, still watching the blade, "and a bunch of rats scurried over and nibbled through it."

"Just our luck," Joe said. "Morslip's a tidy housekeeper. No rats or meat lying around." He tried to steady his nerves. "At the rate it's moving, the pendulum should touch us in about five minutes. I figure it'll get us both right on the waist. Well, I've been meaning to take a few inches off the ol' gut."

"I've got an idea," Frank said. He was staring at the pendulum.

"I hope it's a good one," Joe remarked. "In fact, I hope it's your best. All right, what should we do?"

"Nothing," Frank answered. "Just lie here and wait."

"So far I don't like it," Joe confessed.

"I think it'll work," Frank assured his brother. "Let me concentrate."

Joe started breathing deeply, trying to keep himself together, while Frank continued concentrating on the steady, measured swing of the pendulum.

Soon Frank and Joe could hear a quiet swish each time the pendulum swung—swish-back, swish-forth, swish-back—and the Hardys could see the pendulum was indeed quite sharp.

After what seemed like a year to Joe, the pendulum was swinging less than a foot from his midsection.

Suddenly Frank arched his back and caught the pendulum with his stomach. Pushing upward, Frank was momentarily holding the blade in place!

"Frank," Joe cried in surprise, "isn't it cutting you?"

"No," Frank said with effort. "I've got the floppy disk under my shirt."

"Nice one." Joe let out a long exhale. "But you can't stay like that. It'll cut the plastic soon."

"I've been studying the way the rod's attached to the ceiling," Frank explained. "And it should pivot."

Still pushing upward, using enough pressure to overpower the force of the motor, Frank twisted his midsection and managed to pivot the pendulum to an angle. Still pushing, Frank craned his head to look at Joe's left wrist. He twisted again, adjusting the angle on the pendulum further.

Finally Frank lowered himself and the pendulum began to swing again, but this time it slashed diagonally across Frank and Joe.

Swish-back. Swish-forth. Swish-back.

"I see," Joe observed. "You aimed it for my left wrist, right? So the blade will sever the binding."

"Right," Frank answered.

"No, you mean left," Joe quipped, suddenly feeling better.

"In a few minutes, you'll need to raise your left wrist as high as possible while keeping the rest of your body very still," Frank pointed out. "This is going to be tricky."

After what seemed like another year to Joe, the pendulum was very, very close. "The sound in my ear is starting to sound like a howling wind," Joe whispered nervously.

"All right," Frank coached, "time to lift your wrist and suck in your gut."

"Yes, sir," Joe said, following the orders.

128

Swish—Joe felt the blade graze his shirt, then graze the leather binding. Swish—the blade grazed the leather, then his shirt.

Back and forth the blade went across the leather. Joe felt the blade very close to the critical veins on his wrist as it slashed deeper into the leather.

Then the leather binding split open, and Joe jerked his wrist away. As soon as the blade came back to him, Frank stopped it with his stomach.

"I'm outta here!" Joe cheered as he quickly unbuckled the binding on his right wrist and then both his ankles. "And so are you!" Joe cried as he swung off the table and quickly unfastened all of Frank's binding.

"Thanks," Frank grunted as he released the pendulum. Instantly he rolled off the table.

"That was way too close a call," Joe said, examining the tear in Frank's shirt.

"It's ten minutes till noon," Frank said, checking his watch. "That's when the tournament starts. I'm sure that's where Morslip plans to have the knight strike."

"Well, the only thing stopping us," Joe said, wiping sweat from his face, "is a thick door with a three-inch slab of wood for a bolt."

"We've got some sharp objects and some torches," Frank said, glancing around the room. "Burning the door down could be faster but we might not get out of here alive."

Joe seized a long staff with a pointed blade at the end. "I've decided I like living," Joe said, testing the weight of the staff.

"Certainly better than the alternative," Frank

remarked as he noticed the pendulum slicing into the wooden table.

"And you know what?" Joe said, stalking around the room with the staff, searching for something. "Those monks are really bugging me!"

Suddenly Joe brought the staff crashing down on a tape machine recessed low in the wall, and the chanting stopped.

"Thanks," Frank said. "I think I've had my fill of Gregorian chants for the day."

"Now let's get to work on this," Joe said, moving to the door. He crashed the sharp end of the staff into the wood.

An alarm started shrieking!

Joe kept crashing the staff into the door until the wood began splintering under the blade's point. Soon there was a rough hole in the door. "Take it, Frank," Joe panted, handing the staff to his brother.

Frank began driving the staff through the hole into the wooden bolt on the other side. Before long the bolt broke free, and Frank kicked the door wide open.

Frank and Joe stepped out of the room. "He might still be here," Frank said, straining to listen over the sound of the alarm. "Apparently Carla does all the sabotage at the fair by herself."

"Don't you think he would have come down by now?" Joe pointed out. "We've made a fair amount of racket."

"Who knows?" Frank shrugged as he moved up the basement steps. "He might be waiting upstairs to ambush us with a rifle from the Franco-Prussian

War." Frank tried the door at the top of the steps and found it locked.

"You want this one too, Judo Man?" Joe asked.

"Sure," Frank replied. And with an expertly placed kick, Frank sent the door flying open.

Finding no sign of Morslip in the house, Joe headed for a telephone. "I'm calling Con Riley," Joe said as he dialed. "It's definitely time to bring the police into this medieval nightmare."

Minutes later the Hardys ran out the front door of the house, causing another screaming alarm to go off. They were halfway to the van when they heard someone yell, "Freeze or we shoot!"

Frank and Joe whipped around to see two men in security-guard uniforms running toward them holding pistols.

"We're not burglars," Joe called as he and Frank reluctantly slowed to a stop. "We were held inside that house against our will and we just busted out!"

"On the ground!" one of the guards yelled. "Hands behind your heads!"

Knowing the drill, Frank and Joe both knelt on the ground and folded their hands behind their heads.

"Call the Bayport Police HQ," Frank urged. "Ask for Con Riley. He'll back us up. We're detectives."

"You look pretty young to be detectives." One of the guards smirked, keeping his pistol trained on the Hardys.

"Call him *now!*" Joe shouted. "We've got to get out of here!"

131

The smirking guard nodded, and the other guard trotted over to a parked company car. "It's okay," the guard called after a few moments. "Bayport PD says we can let them go."

"We're just doing our job," the smirking guard said as he holstered his pistol.

"We understand," Frank said, "but we gotta go!"

Frank and Joe dashed to their van, climbed inside, and screeched away from Tommy Morslip's quaint little house of torture.

"It's twelve-thirty," Joe said, checking his watch. "Bayport PD should be there any minute, but we need to be there, too. At least we have some idea how this knight operates. He's pretty devious."

"She," Frank said as he focused on his driving. "The knight's a she."

After pushing the van at breakneck speed for half an hour, Frank barreled into the overcrowded parking lot at Windsor Park. Frank and Joe slammed out of the van and started running for the entrance gate, but suddenly they heard a ping. Then another ping.

"Watch it!" Joe yelled as he and Frank both threw their bodies against a parked car. They heard several more pings. Then a ring of metal.

"Other side," Frank called, and he and Joe dashed to the other side of the car and ducked down.

"Well, we've got a problem," Joe said. "Someone is shooting at us!"

15 Tournament of Champions

"It's got to be Morslip," Frank said, his mind racing. "Maybe the security company sounds his beeper when an alarm goes off at his place."

"He knew we escaped," Joe panted, "so he came to get us here."

"At least the cops are here, too," Frank said, nodding toward the entrance gate, where three police cars were parked.

"But we're the only ones with any real proof against Morslip," Joe said. "If he can take us out, he probably figures he can still get away with this."

Several more pings hit the car, ringing against the metal.

"I think he's somewhere between us and the front gate," Frank said, peering around the car.

"He's probably by his own car," Joe added.

133

"Which means he can chase us if we try to drive around and get in the park somewhere else."

"He won't chase us inside the park though," Frank put in. "He knows the cops are there."

"Stay here," Joe instructed. "I've got an idea."

"What is it?" Frank asked.

"I'll surprise you," Joe called as he dashed back toward the van. Frank stayed crouched behind the car, wincing when he heard a few more pings, but he soon heard Joe slam inside the van.

As Frank and Morslip both waited, Frank heard a great cheer go up inside the park. Some poor knight probably just got bashed off his horse, Frank thought.

After a few minutes, Frank heard several more pings and he spun around to see Joe running toward him. He couldn't help grinning when he saw Joe was wearing his full suit of armor and, across the lot, he thought he heard Morslip laughing. Seconds later, Joe was kneeling beside Frank, lifting the visor on his helmet.

"Good thing I've been keeping my armor in the van," Joe said. "Bledsoe said this stuff was bulletproof."

"Are you *sure* it's bulletproof?" Frank asked.

"Bledsoe said a friend of his tried it," Joe said.

"But Morslip's not using a Colt six-shooter now," Frank countered. "He's using a semiautomatic and he's pretty close."

"We can make it," Joe declared. "We'll run for the gate and you stay on the side of me away from Morslip."

"Remind me to get scared when this is over," Frank said, running a hand through his dark hair.

"I look forward to it," Joe said, lowering his visor. "Let's go!"

As a great cheer sounded from the park, Frank and Joe started racing for the front gate, Frank keeping on the far side of Morslip's pistol. Pings shot through the air as rapidly as popcorn popping at high heat, but the Hardys kept running.

"Are you okay?" Frank called as he ran.

"Yeah," Joe called back. "I think a bullet might have grazed my armor, but I can't really tell."

"Homestretch," Frank called out a few breathless seconds later. "Let's go for it!" And with an extra burst of speed, Frank and Joe dashed straight for the admission gate as a staff member in a serving girl's costume leapt out of the way of the charging Hardys.

The Hardys rushed through the gate as another cheer resounded from the park. "I don't care if you have your own costume," the girl shouted after them, "that'll be twenty dollars!"

"Made it!" Joe cried, throwing up his visor. The Hardys kept racing down a tree-lined path until they were approaching the field, where a great mass of people were gathered. As they hit the field they saw the bold array of costumes and banners and horses and knights—the Tournament of Champions was in progress!

"There will be one final match for this session," King Bertram called to the crowd, "and then we will resume the tournament at five o'clock!"

Frank and Joe stopped at the outskirts of the tournament and glanced around, appraising the situation. "So far everything seems to be okay," Frank said, catching his breath.

"I see four cops," Joe said, noticing four officers moving through the crowd. "And wait, I think I see another way off in the forest."

"This last match," King Bertram declared, "will be between my chief adversary, Sir Damian, and one of my finest knights, Sir Maxwell of Belgrade."

"Sir Maxwell must be one of Bledsoe's jousting buddies," Frank said, looking over the knights in both orange and purple armbands. "And those must be the rest of them."

Frank and Joe noticed five new knights, each wearing genuine metal armor scarred by what appeared to be real battle marks. Beside each knight was a horse draped in a decorative comparison and a squire holding a wooden lance at least eight feet long.

"I'm going to talk to the cops," Joe said, moving away. "Be right back."

Frank watched Sir Damian and Sir Maxwell mount their horses and receive their lances from their squires. The two knights then guided their horses to opposite ends of a low wooden fence about forty yards in length. Overhead the sun was valiantly attempting to break through the clouds.

"The cop tells me," Joe said, returning to Frank, "that all the weaponry and armor were carefully checked right before the tournament. There are eight police officers on the grounds, and they're patrolling the place as if the President were here."

"Knights, prepare to joust!" the herald cried.

Sir Damian and Sir Maxwell both lowered their visors and couched their lances in their arms so the lances ran parallel to the ground. A thrill of excitement ran through the crowd.

The herald blew a loud blast on his horn.

Then, like an explosion, the knights began thundering toward each other, galloping faster and faster until they were just a speeding blur of color and motion. With a violent crash, their lances met. Sir Maxwell's lance snapped in half, and Sir Maxwell was knocked back on his horse, gripping the reins for control.

A mixture of cheers and boos flew up from the crowd. "One strike for Sir Damian of Mandeville!" the herald cried.

"Man, that's exciting!" Joe exclaimed. "These guys are worth every cent they cost!"

"And it looks like it's paying off for Growtowski," Frank added. "There's a tremendous crowd here today."

"I see Iola with the noble set," Joe said, picking faces out of the crowd. "And there's Callie standing among the commoners."

"And Sir Chet's waving to us." Frank chuckled and waved back to his friend, who was standing amid his fellow Avalon knights.

"It looks like the knights are ready for another run," Joe said, noticing Sir Damian and Sir Maxwell back in their starting places. Sir Maxwell had a new lance, and Sir Damian was proudly waving to the crowd.

"Joe, look!" Frank exclaimed, suddenly pointing toward the forest. Through the distant trees, the Hardys could see a galloping black figure, and they knew at once who it had to be.

"Hey!" Joe called to one of the police officers, but then he saw the cops were already on their walkie-talkies, aware of the black-suited invader.

"I don't know what she can do here," Frank warned, "but be ready for anything."

"I'm ready, brother," Joe vowed, adjusting a glove. "I've been waiting for a crack at this guy!"

"Girl," Frank corrected. "Remember, it's a girl."

Suddenly the Knight of the Flaming Sword burst through the trees and began galloping across the vast field. Heads in the crowd turned, and Sir Damian couched his lance, ready to attack. King Bertram glared, as if to will the villainous knight away with his eyes. Frank and Joe saw the officers' pistols come out of their holsters.

Finally the knight reached the crowd, and as he pulled his horse to a halt he also pulled out a small wooden bow. "What's she up to?" Frank wondered as the knight pulled an arrow from a quiver.

"Get off the horse!" one of the cops demanded, aiming his pistol at the knight. "Get off the horse at once!"

Without even glancing at the officer, the knight touched something on the arrow, and flames suddenly ignited around the point. There was an

138

excited gasp from the crowd, most believing it was all part of the show.

"She can't get away with this," Joe murmured as the knight loaded the arrow into the bow.

Suddenly Sir Damian spurred his chestnut horse and began charging straight for the knight with his lance. Quickly the knight aimed the bow, released the bowstring—and a flaming arrow went whizzing past the head of Sir Damian's horse!

With a loud neigh, Sir Damian's horse reared back on its hind legs and threw Sir Damian roughly to the ground. Sir Damian rolled away from the horse's hooves as members of the crowd backed away in fear.

"Watch out, everybody!" Joe yelled as Sir Damian's horse began prancing wildly about.

"Get off the horse at once!" the cop ordered, still aiming his pistol at the knight. "You're surrounded —don't make us use force."

Unimpressed, the knight had another flaming arrow poised to shoot. The knight released the bowstring, and the arrow went sailing straight past the head of Sir Maxwell's approaching horse. The horse bucked then reared, tossing Sir Maxwell to the grass, then it began prancing wildly about Sir Damian's horse.

"She's spooking the horses!" Joe shouted as people rushed away from the out-of-control animals.

"Close in on her!" one of the cops called to the others.

"I can't!" another cop called back. "There's too many people in the way!"

By now the knight had loped to another position and had shot another flaming arrow. With a whinny, another horse began prancing crazily about the field.

Frank saw one of the cops aim his gun in the air, fingering the trigger. "Don't shoot!" Frank called frantically. "It'll just make it—"

Too late! A gunshot split the air! All six horses neighed wildly and began galloping about the field.

People were screaming and scampering to get out of the way, some getting knocked over by the sudden human stampede. The jousters were racing to catch their mounts, but in the confusion the task was almost impossible.

"Hold all fire!" one of the cops called to the one who had fired the gun.

The Knight of the Flaming Sword was now defiantly cantering through the chaos, his horse apparently trained to keep cool in the situation. Joe then saw the knight pull a long and very real sword from a scabbard.

"I'm getting a horse!" Joe called, putting his helmet on.

The knight lifted the sword high into the air, flipped a switch—and flames leapt to life along the sword's blade!

From the ground, Frank swung one of the long lances at the knight, but the knight easily jerked his horse away.

"Will you stop?" Growtowski pleaded as he ran up to the knight.

But the knight was already riding through the crowd, swiping at visitors with the flaming sword.

"Stop him!" Growtowski shouted to Frank. "He's going to set somebody on fire!"

"I'm trying to!" Frank called as he ran after the knight with the cumbersome lance.

"Frank, watch out!" Frank heard Callie scream. Just then one of the spooked horses veered wildly at Frank, knocking him to the ground.

Meanwhile, Joe was desperately running alongside the crazed chestnut horse. He reached out for the reins as he ran, grabbed, but missed.

"Joe, help!" Joe turned to see the knight charging straight for Iola!

Iola began to flee, but the knight quickly bore down on her, slashing at her with the sword. Iola dove to the ground, avoiding the blows.

Joe saw the knight pull his horse around for another try, but another horse pranced by, blocking the knight's path. Seizing the chance, Iola sprang up and made a mad dash for the forest.

More determined than ever, Joe raced after the chestnut horse again, and this time he managed to catch hold of the reins and slow the frightened animal. As he glimpsed the knight galloping after Iola again, Joe swung himself up into the saddle.

"Easy, pal, easy," Joe said, stroking the horse's massive neck to gain its confidence.

"Here!" Chet called, running up to Joe with one

of the rattan swords. Joe grabbed the sword, lowered his visor, and began galloping furiously after the knight.

"Go, Sir Joe!" Chet yelled.

Joe saw Iola's jeweled crown come toppling off her head. The knight pounded after her, trampling the crown, obviously determined to cut down the fleeing princess in pink. Joe flicked his reins and leaned forward, urging his horse faster.

Soon Iola dashed into the foliage of the forest, and Joe lost sight of her. Next the knight galloped into the forest. Joe kicked his horse, pressing it on still faster. He felt his heart pounding in rhythm with the horse's thundering hooves, and soon he saw the greenery of trees rushing past him.

Up ahead, through a maze of trees, Joe caught sight of the fleeing pink gown and the pursuing black armor. Joe kept galloping after them.

Joe then saw Iola glance back over her shoulder, gauging her lead. She crashed smack into a tree trunk!

Iola reeled unsteadily on her feet. Seconds later Joe saw the knight pull up beside her, raising the flaming sword high, aiming to bring it down on Iola's gown!

16 The Chauvency

Galloping frantically, Joe stretched as far as he could in the saddle and took a desperate swing at the flaming sword, knocking it backward.

As Joe slowed his horse, the surprised knight took a second to regain his grip on the sword. Meanwhile, Iola slid down the tree trunk and fell to the ground.

"Iola!" Joe called in horror.

But the knight had pulled his horse around to face off with Joe. The flames had died out on the sword, but the weapon looked deadly enough without them.

Joe swung first, catching the knight's left shoulder with his sword. That should be an amputation, Joe thought, then remembered this wasn't a game. Then, *clang!* The knight swung his sword into Joe's helmet, and Joe's head rang like a fire station alarm.

Stay on the horse, Joe thought dizzily. Hearing his breathing echo loudly inside the helmet, Joe clutched his reins and gripped his sword with his gloved hand.

The knight wheeled the sword high around his head and sent it slashing toward the left side of Joe's helmet. Joe blocked the blow, then slashed furiously at the knight. But the knight's superior sword caught the blow with such force, Joe's rattan sword flew out of his grasp.

Joe quickly edged his horse away to escape the next strike. Meanwhile, the knight guided his horse back to Iola, who was groggily rising from the ground. Joe saw the knight reignite the sword with the flame and reach it toward Iola's gown!

"Carla, stop!" Joe called, throwing up the visor of his helmet. The knight turned to look at Joe.

"It's me," Joe continued, "Joe Hardy. I know all about you and your uncle Tommy. Let's talk about this. Please."

The knight stared back at Joe through the eye slits of his black helmet.

"I know your uncle's been manipulating you," Joe said. "And I think the court will understand this."

The flame went out on the knight's sword.

Iola slowly approached the knight. "They might even understand why you started doing this," Iola dared to say. "I think I do. You felt cheated because they wouldn't let you be a knight. Joe told me about it. I think I even understand why you were after me.

144

I was kind of obnoxious about being a princess when you were stuck being a serving girl."

"Now, why don't you give me the sword," Joe said, gently guiding his horse closer to the knight. "Then we'll do what we can to help you. I promise."

The knight hesitated, then began surrendering the sword to Joe. Then he stopped.

"Come on, Carla," Joe urged. "Chances are you'll get out of this pretty lightly. No jail time at all."

Suddenly the knight held the sword in front of Joe's horse. The knight flipped a switch, and once again flames shot up along the sword's blade!

Frightened by the fire, Joe's horse neighed and wildly jerked back onto its hind legs, tossing Joe violently to the ground.

As Joe's horse began to prance about, the knight spurred his horse and raced away through the forest. Joe pushed himself up and began running to catch hold of his mount.

"Find Frank and the cops," Joe called to Iola as he ran. "Tell them the knight's escaping west!"

"Right," Iola called, dashing off through the trees.

Joe finally caught hold of his horse, swung up onto it, and with a kick went galloping off in pursuit of the knight. As the bark and foliage of the trees flew by with increasing speed, Joe tried to keep his eyes on the figure in black far ahead.

Soon Joe galloped out of the forest, slowing the

145

horse as he moved through a grassy clearing. The knight's horse was calmly grazing, but Joe saw no sign of the knight.

Joe then noticed a fence that bounded the park, and through the wires he saw the knight running toward a black car that was parked on a shoulder of the highway nearby.

Joe surveyed the fence, then guided his horse a good distance back from it. The other day, Joe recalled, he had seen Carla jump this very chestnut horse over an obstacle almost as high. The black car gunned its engine and sped off down the highway.

Joe flicked the reins, and his horse galloped for the fence, the wires rushing closer and closer. The horse lifted Joe up and over the fence, and the two of them landed solidly on the other side.

Steering the horse with his knees and reins, Joe sent the horse galloping along the shoulder of the highway in pursuit of the black car.

It's probably Morslip driving the car, Joe figured, and there's no telling where he's headed.

Joe leaned forward in the saddle, urging the horse onward. The traffic on the road was just light enough to keep the black car in Joe's view.

As a car drove by, Joe saw a man lean out the window to gape at the galloping knight. "Hey, buddy," the man called, "I think you got the wrong century!"

Up ahead the black car found an opening and sped away until Joe watched it disappear on the horizon.

But just then Joe heard a horn honking loudly,

and he turned to see the Hardys' van tearing up the highway, soon slowing to match Joe's pace.

"Morslip's in the black Maxima," Joe called to the van.

"Thanks," Frank called back. "Two hundred horsepower's better than one!"

Frank gunned his engine and flew up the highway, expertly switching lanes to catch up to the escaping black car. Soon Frank was closing in on Morslip, who was now switching lanes at a dangerously high speed.

Morslip recklessly switched to another lane, and suddenly a car slammed into his back fender. Morslip's car went skidding across the highway then hurtled off the road, toppling onto its side. The car took a rough bounce, which popped the hood open. A fire burst out near the engine.

Frank screeched to a stop and rushed over to the crashed car. He yanked the driver side door open and pulled the stunned Morslip from the car. He then reached in farther and hauled out Carla.

Frank escorted Morslip and Carla away from the car as the fire in the hood leapt higher. They seemed too dazed to put up a fight. Soon Joe arrived, swinging off his mount like a champ, and moments later a police car screeched to a halt, its siren blaring.

Before long the fire was extinguished, and Morslip and Carla were in handcuffs beside one of the several police cars now on the scene. After giving the cops some information, Frank and Joe walked over to Morslip and Carla.

The squad car's flashing red light played across the faces of the two crusading villains. Carla no longer wore a helmet, and Joe noticed tears streaming down her cheeks.

"I never wanted to hurt anyone," Carla sobbed.

"Then why did you?" Frank demanded.

"Uncle Tommy talked me into it," Carla confessed. "I went along at first because I was so angry at the fair for not letting me be a knight. But after the first day, when I saw people getting injured, I wanted to quit. But then Uncle Tommy . . ."

"Don't tell them any more," Morslip warned. "Stay brave, kid. Just like Joan of Arc."

"But Uncle Tommy told me," Carla continued, "that he'd turn me in and I'd go to jail. After all, I was the one who was doing all the sabotage. I didn't want to keep hurting people, but I was also terrified of going to jail. So I kept following his orders. Now I guess they're going to burn me at the stake."

"No one's going to burn you at the stake," Joe said, sympathetically touching Carla's arm.

"That's right," Morslip assured Carla. "If you keep quiet, we'll beat this rap, then find another country to conquer." He then turned to the Hardys as if they were old friends. "Maybe you boys will come out to the house again," Morslip invited. "I'm expecting a rifle that was actually shot in the Battle of Waterloo, and I'd love to show it to you."

The cops then ushered Tommy Morslip and Carla into the backseat of the squad car, and soon they were heading off for a long session at the Bayport police headquarters.

"Fun guy," Joe said, watching the police car drive away.

"A regular cutup," Frank stated.

When they returned to the park, Frank and Joe were surprised to see the fair still in full swing. The sun had won its battle with the clouds and was now shining over the hundreds of people milling through the fair and enjoying its activities.

The Hardys soon found Growtowski on the field. "I made an announcement," Growtowski told them, "explaining what's happened here over the past week. I offered refunds to anyone who wanted them but almost everyone refused."

"Any talk of lawsuits?" Frank asked.

"Not to my knowledge," Growtowski answered.

"Do you think you made enough money today to keep the fair open?" Joe asked.

"Yes, he did," Alvin Sing said, approaching the group. "I've been crunching some numbers and it appears Avalon will just about break even for the week."

"And I want to talk to you about your ideas," Growtowski said, draping an arm across Sing's shoulders.

"I hope so," Sing replied. "Because after this week I'm not sure I want my own fair. I'm better behind the scenes, and you, Mr. Growtowski, have proved yourself to be an inspiring leader in battle."

"Well," Growtowski said, tipping his crown, "there must be some reason my first name is Arthur!"

* * *

At five o'clock the Tournament of Champions resumed. After two hours of spectacular jousting and hand-to-hand combat, the tournament came down to the last match between Sir Damian and Sir Maxwell, with Sir Maxwell finally proving himself the victor.

"Noble king," Sir Damian said, kneeling before King Bertram, "my followers and I have suffered defeat today from your valorous knights. As agreed, my knights and I pledge allegiance to you and the honor of Avalon."

"I accept your allegiance," King Bertram said, pulling Sir Damian to his feet. "And now," King Bertram called to the crowd, "it's time to choose the day's Champion of Champions. Though many have shown themselves magnificently today, I deem the honor must go to Sir Joe and Sir Frank of Bayport!"

The crowd cheered and applauded as Frank and Joe modestly made their way up to the king. King Bertram then gestured toward the lake, where a boat was gliding across the glistening water. A man in costume was rowing the boat, and on the prow stood the Enchantress, who was holding aloft a very special sword.

When the boat landed, the Enchantress disembarked and brought the sword to Art Growtowski. Though the weapon was scarred and darkened by time, certain spots revealed the original burnish of its steel.

"This is the Chauvency!" Growtowski proudly

cried, lifting the sword to the sky. "It was owned by a knight of unknown name who lived in the thirteenth century. I had it brought from a museum today in the hope that, like the Excalibur of King Arthur, it would somehow have the power to protect me. And I believe it has."

Enraptured, the crowd stared at the ancient weapon as a beam of sun glinted off the blade. "Sir Joe and Sir Frank," King Bertram commanded, "I bid you kneel."

Frank and Joe both knelt before King Bertram. "I dub you both," King Bertram said, touching them each on both shoulders with the Chauvency, "lifelong protectors of Avalon and the ideal of peace it has always represented."

Frank and Joe then rose, truly feeling an honor had been bestowed upon them. "And now," King Bertram informed the Hardys, "you may each choose the hand of any lady in the land."

Frank saw Callie beaming in the crowd and he walked right over to her and took her hand. Joe, on the other hand, spent some time gazing around, taking in all the ladies in the vicinity.

Joe felt a slap on his armored arm. "Hey," Iola said sharply, "I'm right here."

"Well, then," Joe said with a grin, taking Iola's hand, "I guess I'll settle for the king's daughter."

As the herald loudly blew his horn, Sir Damian and Sir Maxwell began galloping about the field on horseback, triumphantly calling out the words "Long live Sir Joe and Sir Frank of Bayport! Long

151

live Avalon!" As if in answer, the Avalon banner atop the castle snapped and waved bravely in the breeze.

And as a final tribute, Chet came running up to Sir Frank and Sir Joe. "Well, the Hardy brothers were famous before," Chet exclaimed with great pride, "but now you guys are a legend!"